Murder Under A Full Moon

A Mona Moon Mystery
Book Seven

Abigail Keam

Worker Bee Press

Published in the USA by

Worker Bee Press
P.O. Box 485
Nicholasville, KY 40340

Books By Abigail Keam

Josiah Reynolds Mysteries
Death By A HoneyBee I
Death By Drowning II
Death By Bridle III
Death By Bourbon IV
Death By Lotto V
Death By Chocolate VI
Death By Haunting VII
Death By Derby VIII
Death By Design IX
Death By Malice X
Death By Drama XI
Death By Stalking XII
Death By Deceit XIII
Death By Magic XIV
Death By Shock XV

The Mona Moon Mystery Series
Murder Under A Blue Moon I
Murder Under A Blood Moon II
Murder Under A Bad Moon III
Murder Under A Silver Moon IV
Murder Under A Wolf Moon V
Murder Under A Black Moon VI
Murder Under A Full Moon VII
Murder Under A New Moon VIII

Last Chance For Love Romance Series
Last Chance Motel I
Gasping For Air II
The Siren's Call III
Hard Landing IV
The Mermaid's Carol V

1

A white gloved butler opened the door of Mona's silver Rolls Royce and offered his hand to help her and Violet out of the car.

Mona handed him their engraved invitation cards. "I am Miss Mona Moon and my companion is Miss Violet Tate. I believe the First Lady is expecting us for lunch."

"Yes, Miss Moon." He then looked at Violet and greeted her. "Miss."

Violet nervously nodded back while clutching her stomach, which felt like a thousand butterflies were taking flight.

Taking note of Violet's apprehension, the butler gave a ghost of a smile before smothering it. "Come this way, please."

A Marine sentry opened the door to the White

House as Mona and Violet followed the butler into the main hall and stopped before a podium with a registration book. "Please sign in with your name, official title, and town. Mrs. Roosevelt likes to keep a record of all her visitors."

"Of course," Mona replied, bending over to sign the book. She wrote *Miss Mona Moon, Moon Enterprises Owner, Lexington, Kentucky* in longhand. When finished, she handed the fountain pen to Violet.

"Me?"

"You're a guest of Mrs. Roosevelt's, aren't you, Violet?"

"I thought I would be having lunch with the maids in the kitchen."

The butler shook his head. "No, Miss. You both are to dine with the First Lady."

"Oh, dear," Violet said, looking wide-eyed at Mona.

"Just sign. I'll be right next to you throughout the entire luncheon," Mona said.

Violet signed the book, taking care with her letters and writing in cursive. When finished, she handed the fountain pen to the butler.

He replaced the cap and laid it back on the

pedestal. "Follow me, please."

They wandered through several corridors and up one flight in the elevator, whereupon they were shown into a small receiving room.

The butler said, "Mrs. Roosevelt and Mrs. Longworth will join you shortly."

"I see."

"May I pour you a sherry or any beverage of your choice?"

Mona replied, "No, thank you. We're fine."

"Very good then. Just push the button next to the door if you require anything."

"Thank you," Violet said absent-mindedly, taking in the room.

Again, the butler shot Violet a small smile before quietly shutting the door to the room.

"I can't believe we are in the White House!" Violet exclaimed. "And I'm about to meet one of the most famous women in the world."

"Violet, please calm down. I'm nervous, too. I just hope I don't spill anything and embarrass us," Mona said, biting her lip.

"Nervous, Miss Mona?" Violet said, wide-eyed. "Somehow that makes me feel better." She paused, glancing about. "Wouldn't Mr. Thomas love to talk with the staff here? Look at all this lovely furniture and the flower arrangements. So perfect. So regal."

"I've seen nothing yet to throw shame on Mr. Thomas. He runs Moon Manor like a well-oiled machine."

"I didn't mean to suggest he didn't. I just meant that he would love to see how the staff runs things at the White House."

"Sorry, Violet. I'm a little edgy this morning." Mona exhaled and sat down in one of the floral-pattern overstuffed chairs. "Violet. I hear voices."

Violet strained to listen.

Behind the white pocket doors on the other end of the room, Mona and Violet heard raised voices. They both leaned toward the commotion.

"Can you make out who it is?" Mona asked.

Violet tiptoed to the door and pressed her ear against the wood. "It's Alice Longworth and Mrs. Roosevelt. I recognize Mrs. Roosevelt's voice from the radio."

"Well?"

"I can't make out what they are saying, but it sounds rather heated."

The arguing stopped and silence prevailed.

"Oh, dear," Violet said, hopping away from the pocket doors as they were slid back.

In the entrance stood the First Lady of the United States—Eleanor Roosevelt.

Behind her peeked Alice Roosevelt Longworth wearing a velvet shift dyed her signature color of Alice blue. "Hey, Mona, I see that you brought Bucktooth Becky with you."

Violet's eyes narrowed.

The First Lady strode into the room and held out her hand to shake Mona's. In a high-pitched, upper class British accent favored by the East Coast aristocracy, she said, "Hello, my dear, I'm Eleanor Roosevelt. I'm so happy to meet you. Alice has told me of the progressive programs you have established for your workers. I should like to discuss them."

"It would be my honor, ma'am."

"And who is this lovely ingénue?"

"This is my traveling companion, Violet Tate."

Violet struggled to say something, but only a croak escaped her lips. In her dismay, Violet curtsied.

Alice said, "Violet is Mona's maid."

Mona shot Alice a warning look. "Don't start."

Eleanor observed Alice's fallen face. "Ah ha, I see what Alice has been saying about you is true. A pistol. A real firecracker. Not many people would confront Alice so boldly. She is a formidable woman and my most ardent critic, even if she is my first cousin." Eleanor extended her hand to Violet. "Welcome to the White House, my dear."

Violet squeaked, "Thank you very much, ma'am."

The First Lady smiled. "Save the curtsies for the British. They love it."

"Yes, ma'am," Violet said, sheepishly.

"Shall we?" Eleanor beckoned to the room behind them. A table was set for four. "I dislike eating in the main dining room, preferring a more intimate setting. Besides, the dining room staff likes to eavesdrop on my conversations and report to my husband. This way we will have more privacy."

Not knowing if Eleanor was teasing or not, Mona nodded and said, "The table looks lovely."

"Please sit," Eleanor encouraged.

All four women sat at the round dining table.

Mona and Violet waited for the First Lady to take a sip of water before they placed their laced napkins in their laps.

Eleanor rang a small table bell.

"This is beautiful china," Mona remarked, admiring a plate with a dark cobalt border framed by gilded stars on the shoulder. She traced the presidential coat of arms raised in 24-carat gold in the center.

"Mrs. Wilson commissioned this pattern from Lenox of Trenton, New Jersey. Over a thousand pieces were made at the cost of eleven thousand dollars."

Mona remarked, "A fortune, indeed."

"That's ten dollars a plate," Violet said, staring at her plate and now afraid to touch it.

"Yes, indeed. It's because of all the gold used on the china."

"Golly," Violet mumbled, hardly believing she was having lunch off gold plates with three of the most famous women in the United States. She was far from the rolling hills of the Bluegrass now.

Eleanor said, "Unfortunately, many serving pieces are missing now and most of the remaining cups and plates are chipped. Sooner or later, I am going to have to order a new set of china, but I hate to do so during this Depression. I feel it's a frivolous matter, but my husband said we must keep up appearances. After all, Lincoln kept building the Capitol during the Civil War."

"Why don't you use my father's presidential china? It's very pretty," Alice said after telling the server she wanted a gin and tonic.

"I'll have some iced tea, please," Mona addressed the male server before turning her attention back to the First Lady.

Eleanor remarked, "We have the same issue with Uncle Theodore's china. Chipped and missing plates and cups."

"That's a shame," Alice said. "My stepmother had excellent taste. I thought my father's china was the best of the lot."

"Of course, you did, Alice," Eleanor chided.

Alice sniffed at Eleanor before sipping her gin and tonic.

Bowls filled with cold jellied bouillon were placed before the ladies.

Mona tried not to shudder at the cold soup and pretended to partake. "Mrs. Roosevelt, I must tell you how much I admire President Roosevelt's economic policies and the work you do to improve the lives of women and working people. I know from first-hand experience how hard it is to be something other than a teacher or a nurse if a woman wants a career."

"Call me Eleanor, please."

"Mona for me as well."

"I understand you attended university, Mona. I went to Allenswood Academy where I had wonderful teachers, but I always wished I had furthered my education."

"I studied to become a cartographer."

"How was it finding work, especially during the Depression?"

"I was often hired because my employer could underpay and overwork me. There was no law to protect me. And I had to carry a gun to protect my honor. You do what you have to do to survive. That's why your work on behalf of women is so important."

Eleanor leaned back in her chair and fiddled with her napkin. "My dear, I appreciate the vote of confidence. One of my husband's goals is to raise the standard of living for women, but you wouldn't believe the criticism the President has had to endure, even from within his own family." She shot a look at Alice. "Remember that it has only been fourteen years since women won the right to vote. Unfortunately, there are many in both parties who would like to see the 19th Amendment rolled back."

Mona said, "I think the key to get this country back on its feet is getting people back to work, but it's hard to find reliable help if much of the work force is undernourished and illiterate. That's why I have educational and nutritional programs for my employees. I followed Mr. Roosevelt's New Deal philosophy in my own corporation and it has worked."

Alice leaned back in her chair and took out a cigarette from a silver case and tapped its end on the table. "I'm sorry, but I think all these handouts this administration is giving out will only weaken the country. A man should rise up on his own merit. That's not even talking about the national debt Franklin's programs are costing the American people. Who is going to pay for all these programs?"

Not wishing to create discord by criticizing

Alice, Mona thought, *spoken by a woman who has always been wealthy and has never missed a meal in her life.*

Ignoring Alice, Eleanor said to Mona and Violet, "There's so much work to be done. Right now, we are having enormous difficulties, helping farmers in the Midwest. These dust storms are tearing the land apart. No more topsoil. We are getting reports of people dying from what the doctors refer to as 'dust pneumonia.' People's lungs fill up with dust, and they can't breathe. It's just dreadful. Franklin has been meeting with all sorts of agriculture experts seeking recommendations."

"Kentucky's skies have been hazy for months," Violet said, nodding to the server taking away her unconsumed soup.

"Exactly," Eleanor said. "The Dust Bowl problem is engulfing the country and making the economic crisis worse. That's why I'm so interested in speaking with you, Mona. Tell me about your programs. Moon Enterprises is hiring more men, has had no strikes in the past eighteen months, and is making a profit."

"Like I was saying, Moon Enterprises is following the philosophy of the Roosevelt admin-istration. When my uncle made me his heir, I discovered that Moon Enterprises had been mismanaged. We had a high accident rate and morale was very low. We upgraded much of our mining equipment, instituted safety guidelines, and paid above other mining companies."

"Sounds expensive," Alice remarked.

"It is and we are still paying off loans for the upgrade. But as you say, ma'am, we are making a profit this year."

"Once the unions come in, there will be strife and violence. Mark my words," Alice said, looking askance at the salmon salad and bread & butter sandwiches placed before her.

"I understand the concern about unions, but I also see the need for them," Mona said.

Alice harrumped. "Unions are nothing more than fronts for communism to gain ground in our country."

Ignoring Alice, Mona continued. "As for Moon Manor, it was discovered that many of our employees could not read nor write, so we have literacy classes after work hours."

Violet offered, "I got my high school diploma

in one of Miss Moon's programs."

Eleanor asked, "Will you employ these ideas for your fiancé's estate? I understand you and Lord Farley are to be married."

"Lord Farley is in New York right now arranging passage for us. We want his father to meet me before we officially announce our engagement. Let's say we have an understanding."

"I don't see an engagement ring," Alice commented, glancing at Mona's left hand.

Mona said, "I have one, but I will not be wearing it until the engagement is officially announced."

Putting down the unlit cigarette and picking up a bread & butter sandwich, Alice said, "You'll never get the old man's approval, my dear, unless a dowry is produced. Your family is not high enough in the pecking order."

"I'll be gobsmacked," protested Violet, shocked at Alice's insult.

"Oh, I don't mean to be unkind, dear," Alice said. "But if Robert Farley's father approves of this union, your life will change dramatically. You will be expected to plunk down a great deal of

American money into the old man's estate. The English are always desperate for American cash. The fact that you are rich is in your favor, at least."

"Oh, Alice, you are such gloom and doom," Eleanor said.

Now stabbing at her salad, Alice said, "Doesn't mean I am wrong though. You should have seen all of our 'British cousins' come out of the woodwork when I became of marriage age. They were simply ghastly. Mark my words, Mona. Hold tight onto your pocket book."

Mona started to respond, but Alice interrupted her.

"Speaking of the British, it seems that the Prince of Wales has a new mistress."

"How would you know, Alice?" Eleanor asked.

"It seems the American Lady Furness has been replaced by another Yank named Wallis Simpson. Put that in your pipe and smoke it. Huh, I see from your face, Eleanor, you didn't know."

"Again, Alice, how did you gain that information?"

"Read it from an intelligence report."

Eleanor shook her head. "I must tell Franklin to hide those reports when you are in the White House. You know those are for the President's eyes only."

"Then Franklin shouldn't be leaving those files on his desk," Alice said, now lighting up her cigarette.

"Are you going to get married here or across the pond?" Eleanor asked, beckoning to the server for more water.

"We haven't decided yet," Mona answered. Anxious to change the subject, she redirected the conversation. "Mrs. Roosevelt, I mean Eleanor, it was very kind of you to ask us to lunch."

"I have an ulterior motive. I wanted to see what kind of woman you were. Alice told me how you solved a murder in Lexington. She was impressed, and Alice is hardly impressed by anyone. She thought we should meet. One thing about my cousin is that she is politically astute. Oh, I know she has the tongue of a viper, but she has one of the sharpest minds in Washington."

"Thanks, cuz," Alice mumbled, now sipping a Bloody Mary.

"Alice knows her way around Washington and hears everything. One thing we need to rebuild this country is dependable supplies of copper."

Alice said, "That's true. Congressmen talk to me all the time about the need for metals like tin and copper."

"So you see, I needed to meet you and hear your views on things. One of my jobs as First Lady is to make friends with those who can help bring this country out of this economic mire. I hope you understand, my dear."

"I will try to help whenever possible. I love my country."

Eleanor said, "If things go south in Europe, the United States might be called upon to rise to the occasion. We must be ready if that happens."

"Public polls say the American people want to stay out of Europe's affairs and for them to stay out of ours," Alice said.

Before Eleanor could respond, a secretary entered the room. "Very sorry to intrude, but you have a meeting in ten minutes, Mrs. Roosevelt."

Eleanor looked at her wrist watch. "So I do. It was wonderful to meet you and Violet." As she stood, so did Mona and Violet. Alice remained seated, blowing smoke donut holes into the air.

The First Lady clasped Mona's hands. "I wish you a beautiful wedding and hope to meet you again soon."

"Thank you. I look forward to speaking with you again."

Eleanor turned to Violet. "Violet! You be a good girl now. Don't stop at a high school diploma. Get some college accreditations under your belt. Education is the best gift a woman can give to herself."

"Spoken by a woman who was privately tutored all her life," Alice murmured.

"Ignore my cousin. She knows not of what she speaks."

"Yes, Mrs. Roosevelt." Violet couldn't bring herself to call the First Lady Eleanor.

"Do you have a beau?"

"No, ma'am."

"That's good. Learn all you can before you get married. You need pluck and knowledge to engage in this world. Life is not always kind. Continue with your learning."

"I will. Thank you, ma'am."

"Ladies, duty calls, but feel free to stay as long

as you wish and enjoy your lunch."

Mona and Violet said in unison. "Thank you." After Eleanor left, both Mona and Violet sat back down.

The server poured water in their glasses. "Ladies, tea and coffee are on the buffet as well as more sandwiches. Please ring the bell if you need anything. I'll be waiting outside the door to escort you to the main entrance when ready."

"Thank you," Mona replied, folding her napkin and waiting for the server to exit. She leaned back in her chair.

"Well," Violet said. "Mrs. Roosevelt is a very impressive woman."

"Yes, she is," replied Alice. "But she doesn't know a damn thing about food. Wasn't this lunch just awful?"

Mona burst out laughing, nodding her head. "Well, at least the bread crusts were cut off."

"Hush," Violet admonished, looking about. "The servants will hear us."

"You're quite right, Bucktooth Becky. We should leave so we can criticize without any hindrance."

Violet frowned. "Mrs. Longworth, I wish

you'd quit calling me that. I do not have buck teeth, and my name is Violet, not Becky."

Alice leaned forward and peered at Violet. "Are you sure you don't have buck teeth?"

Mona interceded. "Violet, Mrs. Longworth is having you on. Pay her no heed. I certainly don't."

"I don't like to be teased."

"You don't? I used to be teased by my brothers quite a bit in this very home." Alice sighed. "Those were the glory days when my father was president."

Not wishing to hear another Theodore Roosevelt story, Mona rose. "Shall we go?"

"Yes, we should leave this domicile of austerity. Not like when my father was president. Only the best would do. He would have thrown this lunch out the window in a fit of pique and fired the cook. You know it is Henrietta Nesbitt's fault."

Violet asked, "Who is Henrietta Nesbitt?"

"She's a witch Eleanor hired, and she plans these horrid meals for five and ten cents a go. The recipes are even printed in magazines and the papers. We'd have better fare at the nearest soup kitchen."

Mona said, "Mrs. Roosevelt is only trying to help women economize their food budgets with nutritious meals at a very low cost. I admire her for following her own guidelines."

Alice looked smug. "Oh really? Did you enjoy your lunch, Mona? I noticed you didn't eat very much."

Mona sheepishly grinned. "No comment."

"I thought so. Hey, where are you two staying?"

Mona replied, "The Willard."

"Excellent. We'll take my car and have a proper lunch."

"I have my own car," Mona explained.

"That's even better. I really came by taxi, so you can drive all three of us back to the Willard." Alice rose. "Come on, girls. Let's get the lead out."

Mona and Violet exchanged glances before following Alice out.

2

Mona, Alice, and Violet entered the palatial lobby of the Willard Hotel and headed for the dining room. Mona was starving as she had been too nervous to eat breakfast and only picked at her lunch. Once seated, Mona ordered the fillet of sole with fresh asparagus while Alice decided upon braised beef with noodles, and Violet wanted the fried cornmeal mush with bacon.

"You can take the girl out of the South, but not the South out of the girl," Alice mumbled.

"Did I order wrong?" Violet asked.

Alice remarked, "Cornmeal is a lunch for a sharecropper."

"Then why does this fancy hotel have fried cornmeal on its lunch menu if it is so low-down common?" Violet replied, heatedly.

"Because we have a lot of sharecroppers in Congress. That's not saying much for this country."

"You could learn a lot from a sharecropper," Violet snapped.

"I doubt it," Alice replied.

Mona smiled. She was proud of the way Violet was learning to stand up for herself, and Alice Roosevelt Longworth was a formidable opponent. If Violet could take on Alice, she could stand up to anyone.

"I suppose Mona is paying for our lunch, so why not order the most expensive item on the menu like real meat. Get the fish or the beef. Order a steak even," Alice said.

"Am I paying for your lunch, Alice?" Mona teased. "Didn't realize that."

Violet said, "I like fried cornmeal, and that's what I want."

Alice raised an eyebrow. "Okay. Okay. Just trying to broaden your horizons."

"Noted," Violet said, coolly.

Mona ordered a pink champagne cocktail while observing a young, handsome man two tables away reading *The Washington Herald*, but obviously listening to their conversation. He was wearing a beautifully tailored black suit with a silver pocket watch chain hanging from his waistcoat. She decided not to cause a fuss, because people always tried to listen in when they recognized Alice Longworth. Mona thought nothing more about the gauche young man. After she married Robert, she was going to have to get used to living in a goldfish bowl.

"A bit early for you, isn't it?" Alice said, sipping on another gin and tonic, which was her third cocktail of the day.

"I feel like celebrating. It's not every day someone meets the First Lady of the United States."

"May I order a cocktail, Miss Mona?" Violet asked.

"NO!" both Mona and Alice chorused together.

"Girls my age are getting married, let alone having a drink," Violet insisted.

"You're too young to drink or get married, Violet," Mona said. "Wait until you're twenty-one."

"But you drank at eighteen, Mrs. Longworth."

"Yeah, I did, Violet, and look how I turned out," Alice laughed.

Both Mona and Violet joined in.

Alice said to Violet, "I know you think I'm a horrible old prune, but I'm telling you the truth when I tell you to cherish these years and don't be in a hurry to grow up. Don't rush donning a black velvet gown with pearls that a matron would wear. Be a girl as long as you can. And be very careful whom you marry, Violet. I thought I had married the man of my dreams only to come home from visiting my family to find some other woman's bloomers dangling from the bedroom chandelier."

"Oh, my," Violet gasped, her face turning pink. She thought for a moment before asking, "What do you think of Lord Farley?"

"Violet!" exclaimed Mona. "Such a question."

Alice stared at Mona. "I think with a little bit of luck, Mona and Robert should have a happy marriage. Oh, yes, Violet, luck plays into a good marriage."

"At least, you didn't say we were wrong for each other," Mona said, buttering a roll. She sank her teeth into the yeasty bread. "Oh, goodness, this is heaven. I could fill up on these rolls alone."

"What the devil is all that noise?" Alice asked, turning around in her seat toward the dining room entrance.

Shouting and whistle blowing came from the hotel lobby. Several Congressmen, who were lunching, stood and motioned for their wives to move behind them. Violence was not unheard of in Washington, D.C.

"Some sort of serious commotion that's for sure," Mona said, grabbing her purse where her trusty revolver was stashed.

"What's happening?" Violet asked, twisting in her chair as well.

A man, with pomaded black hair and no hat, burst into the dining room followed by two men. "STOP OR I'LL SHOOT!" yelled one of the pursuing men.

The fleeing man stopped, looked about, and seeing two more men come through the kitchen door into the dining room, ran for a window with his arms covering his head.

The man with the gun, fired two shots as Mona, Alice, and Violet ducked under their table.

The shots missed and the running man jumped through a closed window spraying broken glass over the dining room guests as women screamed. Mona and Alice jumped up and ran to another window. They saw the black-haired man lying prostrate on the pavement outside the hotel. He was not moving.

"Looks like he's been cut to ribbons from the glass," Mona said. "We should get a doctor."

Alice grabbed Mona's arm. "Don't get involved, Mona." She pointed to the four men now outside inspecting the injured man. A car pulled up, and the four men lifted the injured man and put him inside the car. As the car drove off, the four men reentered the hotel.

"I'm going to give those men a piece of my mind," Mona said, heatedly. "Shooting in a room full of innocents. Well, that kind of thing is simply not done."

Alice cautioned, "Mona, listen to me. Those men were G-men."

"You mean they were FBI?"

"Exactly. If for some reason, they want to interview you, only respond with a yes or no. Don't volunteer information. You don't want to come under Hoover's scrutiny. He's one of the most powerful men in Washington."

"Who was the man they were chasing?"

"I don't know. Listen, dear, lunch is over. Have your meal sent up to your room," Alice said, watching other rattled guests leave.

"What about you?"

"I'll be fine, Mona. I'm Alice Roosevelt Longworth. No one bothers me." Alice kissed Mona on the cheek. "If I don't see you again before you leave, have a pleasant journey. Send me a wire every so often. I need to know what is happening with you."

Alice tapped on their table under which Violet was still hiding. "Have a memorable sea voyage, Bucktooth Becky. Say hello to King George for me." With that, Alice strode out of the dining room.

Mona peered under the table. "Violet, I think the drama is over. You can come out."

Violet crawled out from under the table as the manager came over. "Miss, the dining room will be closed until further notice. We need to replace the window and clean. Hopefully, we will be open for dinner. I want to apologize for this unfortunate incident."

"Is the kitchen closed?" Violet asked.

"No, miss. Shall I send your meals to your rooms?"

"That would be wonderful," Mona replied. "We are Miss Moon and Miss Violet in Suite 204."

"I'm afraid there has been a mishap on the second floor. You have been moved to a larger suite on the fourth floor."

Irritated, Mona said, "This is most unusual. I don't like strangers going through my things."

"I completely understand, but I'm afraid it cannot be helped. The entire second floor has been cordoned off until further notice. We have assigned a butler and a maid to help you with the transition. They have been with the Willard for many years and are trustworthy."

"Who was the man that jumped out of the window?" Mona asked.

"I'm not at liberty to discuss the incident. I'm very sorry."

Mona sighed. "I see. Very well then. May we have our keys to the suite?"

"You will find Mr. Hammond waiting for you in your suite. He will serve your lunch, and he also has your keys. It is Suite 432.”

“Who else has keys to our suite?”

“Both Mr. Hammond and the maid have pass keys. And our office keeps another key in case of an emergency.” He motioned to a bell boy. “Jason will escort you to your new suite.”

“No thank you. We can find it on our own. Come Violet.”

Giving a fleeting embarrassed smile at the manager, Violet hurried to join Mona, who was quickly leaving the dining room. “What is going on, Miss Mona? Are we going to take the suite?”

“I don’t know, but I think I’ll put in a call to Robert.” She looked at her watch. “He should know about this incident. I’ll call this afternoon. Violet, I think we should move to a new hotel tomorrow.”

“I can pack our steamer trunks tonight.”

Mona and Violet found their new suite quickly, and just as the manager had promised, lunch was waiting for them on a lace-covered table with white porcelain china encircled by a gold rim with sterling silver serving ware.

Lunch was delicious!

3

Mona was finishing dressing for a party at the British Embassy that evening. She was sure Robert had something to do with the invite. Since he was not able to escort her, Mona was hesitant to attend, but Robert assured her that she would be assisted by an old university friend of his, Colonel Maynard Pickard.

Violet helped Mona slip into her silver metallic backless dress. The front of the dress rose to Mona's neckline in a triangle from the waist only to have it fastened around her neck. Halfway down the back, a silver mesh band reached from side to side keeping the dress in place. The skirt was form fitting and accentuated Mona's hips, flaring out above the knees to accommodate dancing. After checking the dress for flaws,

Violet buckled the ankle straps on Mona's open-toed platinum dress shoes. "There," Violet said, standing back and admiring. "Pretty as a picture."

"I really don't want to go and leave you here alone. Especially after what happened today," Mona said.

Violet replied, "I'll be fine. Lord Farley must have a reason if he wants you to go to this fancy bash."

"Yes, but I have no idea what it is," Mona said, putting on red lipstick. She turned to Violet. "Is my face right?"

"Looks good, but put a little more powder on your nose. It's shiny."

Looking in a mirror, Mona powdered her nose. "Thank you."

A loud knock sounded on the door of the suite.

"That must be your car."

"I don't think so, Violet. The front desk said they would call the suite. Ask who it is before opening the door."

Violet went to the foyer of the suite, which was laid out more as a two bedroom apartment. "Who is it, please?"

"We want to speak with Miss Moon."

Violet looked at Mona, who was standing in the doorway of her bedroom.

"Who *is* we?"

"Wait a minute, Violet." Mona went to get her gun from her purse and motioned Violet to stand away from the door. "Violet, go into your room and lock the door."

"I will not!"

"Then call the front desk and have them send up the house detective."

They both heard the door unlock from the hallway and as the door swung open two men wearing brown Fedoras stepped inside. Upon seeing Mona holding a gun on them, one of them with a scar on his right hand said, "Hold it, sister. We're the good guys. Let me get my badge out." He reached into his pocket and pulled out his credentials. The other man with gray hair, grabbed the phone from Violet and said into the mouthpiece, "Sorry, Mac, there's been a mistake," before hanging the phone up.

Mona still did not lower her gun.

Frightened, Violet rushed to stand beside her.

Mona asked briskly, "What do you want?"

"Someone needs to see you."

"Who?"

"Come with me and you'll see."

"I'm not going anywhere with you."

"Listen, someone important wants to see you and we've got to deliver. It's on the up and up. You can bring your gun with you."

"Why does this person want to see me?"

"Don't know. Wasn't told, but it's government business. If you resisted, I was to tell you that you told Mrs. Roosevelt this morning that you loved your country and wanted to help. Well, now's your chance."

Mona was stunned. She had indeed said that at the luncheon with Mrs. Roosevelt. How would these cretins know this if Mrs. Roosevelt hadn't repeated what she had said?

Still seeing Mona hesitating, the scarred man said, "Look, lady. We're only going a couple of doors down on this floor. You can keep your gun, but we've got to hurry." He shot a look at Violet, "My partner is going to visit with you while Miss Moon is gone to make sure you don't call anyone. This has to be on the down low. You understand?"

Wide-eyed, Violet nodded.

The gray-haired man said, "Please sit." He pulled out a chair for Violet.

"Miss Mona? What should I do?"

"You go downstairs to the lobby, Violet, and if you don't see me in fifteen minutes, notify the front desk that I have been kidnapped."

The gray-haired man blocked Violet's movement toward the suite door.

Mona stomped her foot to gain the man's attention. "This gun is loaded with a hair trigger. You either do it my way or not at all."

The man with the scar jerked his head toward his partner. "Let her leave."

"The boss is not going to like this."

"But what can we do?" He spoke to Violet. "Hey, girlie, take a hike."

Violet shot one last desperate look at Mona before scurrying out of the suite.

Mona motioned to the two men with her gun. "Let's go. Stay six feet in front of me."

The two men sauntered out of the suite and turned right. They stopped four doors down where the men pointed at a door.

Mona said, "Beat it. I'll take it from here."

"Gladly," said the gray-headed man, pushing back his Fedora. They both heard the elevator door ring and dashed for it. A woman with a small dog got off and walked past Mona, who hid her gun in the folds of her dress. As soon as the woman passed, Mona opened the door and walked in.

Near the room's fireplace sat an older man in formal attire smoking a cigarette. He was very well groomed with manicured nails and clipped eyebrows. That went for his hair as well. Mona knew he'd had a haircut that very day as the back of his neck was freshly shaven. His cologne was mild and not overpowering like some men's. His shoes were handmade. Probably Savile Row. The creases in his black tux were crisp. His white shirt was starched. This was a man who took care of himself and bought the very best.

"Good evening, Miss Moon. Would you please have a seat? I won't take up much of your time. I know you will be attending the ball at the British Embassy. I am also attending and meeting my wife there, so I can't tarry long." He glanced at Mona's gun. "You can put that away. You're quite safe."

Mona looked about the room. "Anyone else here?"

"Just us." He took out his silver cigarette case and offered a cigarette to Mona. "Would you like one?"

"No, thank you. I don't smoke."

"Neither do I, really. Just habit here and there." He waved his hand to a chair. "Please sit. What I've got to say should only take a few moments." He gave her a long, hard look. "It's true what they say about you. Your hair is white as snow and your eyes are yellow like a cat's. I guess you know you have an uncanny resemblance to Jean Harlow."

Ignoring the flattering comments, Mona asked, "Who are you?"

"My name is William Donovan."

"Who were those goons who abducted me?"

Donovan tsked tsked. "Abduction is such a strong word and not appropriate. They escorted you, Miss Moon. From time to time, I am allowed the help of FBI gentlemen."

"You call them gentlemen? Those G-men scared my companion half to death."

"But you kept your head. You are completely

unharmed, are you not?"

"Okay, what do you want?"

Donovan explained, "I represent a loose collection of businessmen and lawyers who travel quite extensively. While we are on our travels, we can't help but notice things."

"What kind of things?"

"Anything that might be of use to our government."

"By noticing, you mean spying?"

"I call it information collection, but if you want to call it spying, so be it."

Lowering her gun, Mona asked, "What's this got to do with me?"

"It is rumored that you are going to marry Lord Farley."

"What of it?"

"You will be rubbing elbows with British royalty then. You'll be privy to private conversations of the British aristocracy."

"I doubt that I'll be invited to meet the King and Queen. Lord Farley hasn't seen the royal family for years. He is a noble, not a royal."

"But he does have impressive connections in Great Britain and abroad. So do you. You are great friends with Lady Alice Morrell, whose life you saved in Mesopotamia. You are also an ally of Alice Longworth. I say it is impressive that you are pals with two of the most famous Alices in the English-speaking world."

"So what?"

"There is a concern about Prince Edward's fascination with fascism."

"Who's concerned?"

"His father, King George, for one thing. President Roosevelt for another. There have been intelligence reports that the Prince of Wales' current mistress, Wallis Simpson, is making dangerous friendships and having affairs with men of ill repute while she is seeing Prince Edward. We believe her to be a Nazi sympathizer. We fear her influence over the Prince of Wales might not be in the United States' interest. We cannot allow Great Britain to fall under a fascist government if Prince Edward should become king."

"That's ridiculous. Germany is a constitutional republic with President von Hindenburg at the helm. Nazism is not supported by the majority of the German people."

"That's where you're wrong, Miss Moon. You're not keeping up with current events. The Nazis got almost forty-four percent of the German vote in March of 1933. That's up from eighteen percent of the vote in 1930. The Nazis are very much in control of Germany."

"Hitler made a speech last year at the Reichstag, where he promised continued disarmament and peace."

Donovan produced a condescending smile. "Now, Miss Moon, I know you are an intelligent woman. Surely you're not falling for those lies. Your daddy must have taught you that you go by what a man does rather than what he says. Fascism is gaining ground in Europe. Look at Italy with Mussolini. Stalin in Russia. Oswald Mosley in Great Britain. Von Hindenburg is a frail old man. He won't be able to contain Adolf Hitler for much longer. When he dies, the facade of German democracy will crumble."

"You're right. I haven't been keeping up. I've been trying to turn my little corner of the world around. I haven't had the time to study international politics except in broad strokes."

"I feel Hitler is a very dangerous man and fear

his stranglehold on Germany. I also fear this strain of politics in our own country. It's very easy for people to fall under the allure of a man who has charisma and promises a way back to greatness in times of immense stress. America must stay alert."

"That may be, but I do not see what that has got to do with me. I am not a fascist or a Nazi. I believe in democracy."

"You might hear or see something that will be of interest to our government. The best information gathering service in the world is the Vatican. The second best is MI6 for Great Britain."

"Again, so what?"

Donovan said, "What I'm trying to say is that the United States has no formal organization to gather and sift through information, nor do we have operatives overseas. We do have military gatherings, but the information is not shared. Often, President Roosevelt is not officially briefed on important matters. So, our government currently relies on people such as myself and hopefully, you, to fill in the gaps."

Mona was horrified. "You're asking me to spy

on Lord Farley's family and friends. This I will not do. I am amazed that you would ask me to hand over scraps of gossip that I overhear in the powder room."

Donovan snuffed out his burning cigarette. "You were there when a man jumped out of a window in the Willard's dining room this afternoon?"

"I was." Mona sat down in a chair opposite Donovan. She was very interested now in what Donovan had to say.

"That man's name was Juan Garcia. He is a double agent working for the British government and was attempting to steal a German's attaché case from the man's room when he was caught. He had to kill the German, who worked for the German Embassy."

Mona pulled back.

"You seem shocked."

"I am."

"The FBI has been watching this German agent for a long time. He stayed at the Willard quite often. We believe he was meeting with an American who feeds him information, but we don't know whom. We couldn't catch them in the act of exchanging information. After Garcia began following him, the FBI was given orders to observe and not interfere. Only when Garcia killed the German, did the FBI decide to intervene on Garcia's behalf. But Garcia misunderstood their intentions and put up a fight. He thought our men were enemy agents trying to apprehend him for stealing the case. We finally got hold of him outside the Willard and safely whisked him away."

"Yes, I saw. It was a very clumsy attempt to help. Not subtle at all, especially when your men were shooting at him, and he jumped out a closed window."

Donovan shrugged.

"What happened to the German operative?"

"His body has been taken aboard an ocean liner returning to Germany where he will have a tragic accident of falling overboard and drowning. The body will not be recovered."

"I suppose there will be witnesses saying they saw him fall over the railing."

"Of course."

"What was in the attaché case?"

"Proof that Hitler has no intention of honoring the disarmament clause of the Versailles Treaty."

"He means to build up the German military again?"

"That's what President Roosevelt fears. There is a great deal of sympathy for this Hitler in our country. Many Americans agree with him and his brand of hatred. This could mean disaster to our way of life if a pro-Nazi candidate became president, which may happen when Prince Edward becomes king. People will be influenced by Prince Edward's political bent as he is so popular in our country. For the good of all, the United States must stay the course of being a constitutional republic. So you see, we need everyone doing their part. That's why Mrs. Roosevelt called me to speak with you. She was very impressed with you and felt you could help." Seeing Mona's conflicted face, Donovan stood and looked at his watch. "Your friend, by now, is walking to the front desk and going to inform them that you have been kidnapped. You need to intercept her before our little chat becomes an incident."

"How did you know about that?"

"I heard everything that was said in your room. Remember, the rooms have ears."

"I don't like being spied upon, Mr. Donovan."

"You're no longer Mona Moon the cartographer. You're Mona Moon, one of the wealthiest women in the world, who owns most of the copper mines in the United States. You are going to marry an important man. You must expect people to scrutinize you. Believe me when I say the moment you stepped on the train to come to Washington, you were being shadowed."

"That is disappointing to hear. I was hoping to take a few days here just as plain old Mona Moon and be a tourist like everyone else."

"That is very naïve of you, Miss Moon. Plain old Mona Moon would not have lunch with Eleanor Roosevelt. The rules of the game have changed for you. You see? If I were in your place, I would beef up my security team. You are too vulnerable."

"I don't know what to say, Mr. Donovan."

"Here's an example. I was dining at the Willard the same time as you. I saw you come in with Alice Longworth."

"I didn't notice."

"That's my point. You also didn't notice a blond young man with Nordic features and wearing a dark suit surveilling you."

"I did notice him."

"He followed you and your companions into the dining room. You should have had him checked out. We certainly did. He could be a danger to you. As it is, he is a Swedish diplomat with ties to the Nazi party. I imagine that he is going to contact you to arrange the purchase of Moon Enterprises' copper for his country, but the copper will really be diverted to Germany for their rearmament program."

Mona felt the heat rise to her cheeks. She knew this man was right. She was no longer a private citizen who could do as she pleased. "Mr. Donovan, I feel rather naive."

"Does that mean you will help us?"

"I don't know. I must think on it, but I can assure you that I will be more aware in the future. I would not knowingly do anything that puts my country in jeopardy."

"Whatever you decide, our conversation must be confidential. You can't tell your companion or your fiancé what was discussed between us. I trust you understand the need for secrecy in this matter."

Mona didn't reply, looking gloomily at Donovan. She felt a heavy burden had been placed on her shoulders.

"Think about what I said. That's all I ask." He picked up his hat. "See you at the embassy ball." He strode out of the room leaving Mona alone.

Thinking she better hurry to Violet, she took the stairs down to the main floor while Donovan captured the elevator. Mona caught Violet's hand just as the young girl was reaching for the front desk bell to summon a clerk.

"Oh, Miss Mona. I was so worried."

Mona heard the elevator bell ding. The elevator opened, and Mr. Donovan exited it with aplomb, making his way outside of the hotel. Mona picked up a newspaper from the hotel's front desk and used it to shield her face. She didn't want anyone reading her lips. "Violet, I want you to put in a call to Dexter Deatherage tonight. Tell him to send Jamison and Samuel plus four Pinkertons to me. I also want Rupert Hunt recalled from the West. They are to come to Washington as soon as possible."

"What has happened, Miss Moon? You wanted to be incognito on this trip. No muss. No fuss."

"I'm afraid that is now impossible. I need you to do something else for me, Violet. I want you to use a pay phone away from here to make the call. Reverse the charges. Don't use the hotel's phones. Someone might be listening in from the switchboard."

Violet's mouth shaped into a silent O. "I'll find a telephone that has a privacy box so no one can overhear me."

"There's a drug store around the corner. It's only a block away. Make sure you cover your mouth when you speak."

"I'll go now while it's still light."

"Good girl. Now, I must be off. And not one word about this to Lord Farley if he calls."

"No, ma'am."

"Be careful, Violet."

"You're giving me the chills, Miss Mona."

"I feel slightly cold myself. See you later tonight." Mona strode out of the hotel and asked the doorman to hail her a cab. She tightly clutched her purse, which held her gun, hoping she would not have to use it tonight.

But then again, the evening was young.

4

"Miss Moon?"

"Yes," Mona said, handing her wrap to a maid. She turned and was greeted by an affable man with sandy brown hair and a pencil thin mustache that was now so fashionable.

"I am Colonel Maynard Pickard. It is my honor to be your escort this evening."

Mona smiled and extended her hand, looking him over carefully. His description matched what Robert had portrayed, and Pickard was wearing a red carnation as a signal that he was indeed Pickard.

Pickard swooped Mona's hand up, kissing it in the Continental manner. "Shall I show you to a table?"

"I'd like to meet the British ambassador first.

Where is the receiving line?"

"Let me show you." He offered his arm. "Shall we?"

"Yes." Mona was a little nervous. She didn't want to make a mistake and have it reported to Robert that she had made a faux pas.

Pickard showed her to the line. "I'll get us some drinks. Champagne to your liking?"

"Yes, thank you," Mona replied. She did like champagne, but wouldn't drink what Pickard handed her. She never imbibed any beverage anyone gave her unless it was her staff or Lord Farley. She had seen too many girls taken advantage of that way.

Hearing a commotion, Mona turned to see Alice Longworth had arrived and was causing a stir among the other guests. She was wearing a chiffon dress colored her signature blue with an amazing headdress of ostrich feathers and carrying a fan made of the same.

Mona shook her head, grinning. Alice always liked to make an entrance. Mona moved forward in the line until she felt a tap on her shoulder.

"Thought I would see you here."

"Hello, Alice." Mona pushed a floating ostrich

feather away from her face. "Where did you get that crazy hat?"

"Got it for my twentieth birthday. I'm going to wear it until all the feathers fall out."

"I don't think you have long to wait." Mona picked up another floating feather and handed it back to Alice. "Maybe you can glue that back on."

"What are you doing standing in this line?"

"I'm in the receiving queue for Ambassador Lindsay."

"Standing in line is for mere mortals. Not for the likes of you and me." Alice grabbed Mona's hand and pulled her toward the front of the line. "Excuse me. Excuse me."

Embarrassed, Mona turned to the person they had cut in front of. "I'm so frightfully sorry. Really, I am."

"Mona, pay attention," Alice snapped. "Ronald, I'd like to introduce you to Miss Mona Moon. She is the owner of Moon Enterprises and is filthy rich. Besides that, her mines produce copper ore. Make her your best friend."

Mona felt her face turn bright red. With platinum hair and yellow eyes, she must look a fright—red, white, and yellow. "Ambassador Lindsay, so nice to make your acquaintance. I'm so sorry about this."

The ambassador shook Mona's hand. "Don't worry, my dear. Alice pulls these pranks all the time. We just ignore her."

"Like hell you do," Alice ribbed.

"May I introduce you to my wife, Lady Lindsay."

Mona turned to a middle-aged woman who scrutinized Mona with such intensity Mona felt almost naked. She was sure Lady Lindsay disapproved of her metallic, backless dress. Mona bobbed her head. "Lady Lindsay. It's a pleasure to meet such a noted landscape artist. I have read your treatise on roses and tried to copy your garden plan, but I admit I was a failure. I just don't have a green thumb."

"Perhaps you are not using the right kind of manure."

"Don't be snotty, Elizabeth." Alice warned. "I underestimated Miss Moon once. It's a mistake I shan't make again."

"I understand you are friends with Lady Alice Morrell," Mona said to Ambassador Lindsay.

"You know Lady Alice?"

"Yes, she is my great friend. We met when I was mapping in the Near East and her father was stationed there."

"There's another Alice in your life?" Alice Longworth mocked. "I feel so betrayed."

"Are you the woman who helped Lady Alice escape the rebellion?" Lady Lindsay asked, looking more kindly at her.

"I would say we helped each other out of a difficult situation."

Ambassador Lindsay said, "She wrote to us about the escape and her father's death. It was tragic. Yes, very tragic."

"I understand she has married," Lady Lindsay said.

"She married a Professor Ogden Nithercott. I was fortunate to help them celebrate their marriage at my home, Moon Manor, in Kentucky."

"We must talk soon," Lady Lindsay said. "So very nice of you to come."

Mona realized that was a polite dismissal. They were taking up too much time in the line. "Thank you."

Mona grabbed Alice's arm and guided her away from the hosts.

"You're pinching me. It hurts," Alice complained.

"Good. How could you embarrass me like that?"

"Embarrass you? I made you. Now, they will remember you, and I bet Ambassador Lindsay will cable the prime minister tonight to get permission to discuss the purchasing of copper ore before you leave Washington. And her highness, the Lady Lindsay, will summon you to tea. Why do you think Lord Farley wanted you to come to this party tonight? To nibble hors d'oeuvres and sip pink champagne with another man as your escort? Lord Farley is thinking about the future and that future includes copper ore."

Mona was stunned that Alice would think her marriage to Robert had practical dimensions other than true love, but this was the way the upper class thought. Their marriages were basically strategic alliances. Did Robert think the same way? Would he be interested in her if she was just plain Mona Moon, an out-of-work cartographer? Mona pushed that notion out of her mind. It was too horrible to contemplate.

"Oh, I see that I have shocked you. Mona, listen to my years of experience. I married a politician. If Nicholas had lived, he might have been president, but they are all monsters at heart."

"Robert isn't a politician."

"Oh, really? When his father dies, Robert will become a member of the House of Lords. Expect a great change when that happens. No matter how liberal you think Robert is now, he will always use the law to protect the interests of his class."

"President Roosevelt doesn't."

"Franklin is an anomaly and is despised by his own kind. I can't tell you how many of the family won't receive him anymore. Both Eleanor and Franklin have paid a high price advocating for the common man."

"This looks like a serious conversation. Shall I go away?"

Mona and Alice looked up to Colonel Maynard Pickard holding two glasses of champagne.

"How long have you been eavesdropping?"

Mona asked, reaching for a glass.

"Excuse me?" Pickard said, looking a bit angry at Mona's accusation.

"What Mona wanted to say is that she wants you to dance with her, but since I'm older, I get first dibs," Alice said, hoping to defuse the situation. "You won't say no to the daughter of a former president, would you?"

"Of course not, Mrs. Longworth."

"See there, Mona. Everyone knows who I am. Even this young Englishman whom I've never met."

"This is Maynard Pickard, my escort for the evening. He is a friend of Lord Farley's. Mr. Pickard, this is Alice Roosevelt Longworth."

Pickard clicked his heels and bowed his head. "Everyone knows Mrs. Longworth."

"Of course, they do." Alice took the other champagne flute from Pickard and handed it to Mona. "Shall we?"

Pickard offered his arm after which he and Alice moved gaily to the dance floor as Pickard kept slapping ostrich feathers away from his face.

Left alone, Mona felt devastated. So far, she had embarrassed herself in front of the Ambassador and his wife, argued with Alice Longworth, and insulted Robert's friend, Colonel Pickard. This was not a successful night. She could only imagine what Maynard Pickard would relate to Robert.

"Madam, may I speak with you?"

Mona turned to see the young blond man who had been watching her in the Willard dining room. "Are you following me?"

"Yes, I am."

Startled by the young man's bold confession, Mona laughed, "Well, that's honest."

"I have been trying to find you alone so that I might speak with you."

"Why didn't you make an appointment?"

"I did call Moon Enterprises, but they said you were on holiday and unreachable. Then I saw in the paper that you had come to Washington. I thought if I followed you, I could steal an opportunity to speak with you."

"What do you want?"

The man took the flutes of champagne Mona was holding and placed them on a side table. "My name is Lars Dardel. I work for the Swedish Embassy. Here is my card."

Mona looked at his card. "Still, what do you want?"

Dardel took Mona's elbow and escorted her to the outside patio where men were relaxing with glasses of bourbon and cigars. Dardel pulled up two chairs and turned them away from the men to face the garden Lady Lindsay had planted. "Very sorry for the subterfuge, but the walls have ears." He pulled out a cigarette case and offered one to Mona.

She waved them away. "No, thank you. I don't smoke."

"Please do. Otherwise, it will be asked what you were doing with me if not to smoke."

"All right, but who will be asking?" Mona took a cigarette from Dardel's case and noticed the inscription—*Forever, EMD*. Mona allowed Dardel to light her cigarette.

He lit one up as well.

"Now what's this all about?"

Dardel looked about. "Please lower your voice." Seeing that no one was overtly watching them, Dardel said, "I am assigned to Ambassador Wollmar Boström. Do you know him?"

"No."

"I work in many capacities for the Swedish government. One of my tasks is to obtain certain items that Sweden needs."

"And right now Sweden needs copper ore."

Dardel looked surprised. "How did you guess?"

"There seems to be a great deal of demand for copper ore these days."

"I've been appointed to undertake negotiations for the purchase of copper."

"Why would you want American copper when Sweden produces most of the copper and iron for Europe? Sounds like Sweden wants to corner the market on mineral sales. That could cause further economic chaos. I'm afraid I couldn't allow that."

"I am surprised you know so much about Sweden."

"I know about my company's competitors."

"So you will not sell to Sweden?"

"I'll make that decision when I'm asked officially by Sweden's government."

"Would you consider selling copper to Germany?"

"Are you an agent asking on behalf of Germany?"

"I'm just asking."

Mona drew back in her chair.

Dardel's eyes grew feral as he waited for her reply.

Believing that whatever answer she uttered would be reported back to someone, Mona put out her cigarette and rose. "Thank you, Mr. Dardel, for such an interesting conversation, but I must get back to my escort. No doubt he'll be wondering where I have wandered off to." She wanted to get away from this handsome young man. His congenial demeanor was at odds with the predatory expression on his face. Mona suddenly felt in need of a shower.

Dardel rose and bowed his head. "My pleasure, Miss Moon. It's been an exacting discussion. We shall meet again."

"I hope not," Mona murmured as she went back into the ballroom.

Alice had been right. The avenues of power in Washington, D.C. would follow her wherever she went. She made her way to the open bar and got a flute of champagne watching the bartender pour it. Then she went in search of Alice and Maynard Pickard. She found them huddled in a corner hovering over plates of food.

"May I have some? I'm famished," Mona declared.

Alice slid a plate filled with hors d'oeuvres over to Mona. "Don't worry. No one has sneezed on them."

Mona picked up some crackers with cheese and radish rosettes.

"They have tea sandwiches, Miss Moon. I think cucumber and pimento. I even think there are little biscuits stuffed with smoked ham."

"This will be fine, Colonel Pickard."

"Call me Maynard, please."

"Maynard, it is."

Alice said, "We have been having the most marvelous time. What have you been doing?"

Mona wanted to tell Alice about Lars Dardel and his inquiry about the ore, but decided not to. Alice was a notorious gossip. "Meeting people. Watching people."

"Didn't that nice looking Viking ask you to dance?"

"No, he just wanted to chat for a moment."

"About what?" Alice asked, intrigued.

Trying to distract Alice from prying, Mona

said, "Look, there he goes."

Lars Dardel was dancing with a splendid creature in a red sequined halter top dress. Her curvy figure had all the men looking enviously at Dardel. They were cutting quite a rug. Dardel's hand slipped down the woman's bare back and onto her buttocks. Embarrassed at Dardel's indiscretion, Mona and Alice looked away. They missed seeing the woman step back from Dardel in a fury and storm away to rejoin her escort. Dardel was left standing on the dance floor looking like a fool.

"Who's that?" Alice asked.

"A new starlet from London. She's on her way to Hollywood. I can't quite remember her name," Maynard said.

Hearing that the woman was an actress, Alice lost interest and turned her attention back to Mona. "No one has asked you to dance?"

Mona shook her head.

"Colonel, you must address this at once. What's wrong with the men here?"

"I think they might be intimidated, Miss Alice. Miss Mona is wearing a spectacular dress. It makes men think she is unobtainable especially with all these sour wives around."

"Then we must put a stop to that nonsense," Mona said, smiling. "Take me for a spin. Let's give Dardel and his beautiful partner a run for their money."

At that moment, Ambassador Lindsay approached the table.

Colonel Maynard stood. "Ambassador."

"Sit. Sit. No need for formality. This is a party, after all. I came over to see if one of you charming ladies was in need of a dance partner."

Alice said, "Ronald, you couldn't have picked a better night for this ball. Did you order the full moon to twinkle over Elizabeth's garden? The embassy grounds glisten in the moonlight."

Ambassador Lindsay grinned. "It is a brilliant full moon, I must say, but I had nothing to do with it. Even the British ambassador can't order the moon about. I will tell you a gardener's secret though. Elizabeth had the garden misted with water so the moon's light would reflect off the water droplets."

"Clever," Mona said, impressed.

"Well, ladies, which one of you lovely sirens will take me up on my offer to dance?"

"I've been dancing all evening, so my dogs are

tired. Mona, here, has been a little wallflower. She's in need of a whirl and a twirl around the dance floor if only to show off that dress."

"I must say Miss Moon does sparkle like my wife's garden. Are you keen, Miss Moon?"

"I am, Ambassador."

"Splendid." He crooked his arm toward her.

Mona let Ambassador Lindsay escort her to the dance floor where they did a slow foxtrot.

"You're a very good dancer, Miss Moon."

"Thank you. I've been to more dances in the past year than in my entire life."

"Don't you like parties?"

"I don't like surprises and something unexpected always happens at a party."

"You're not going to like this then." Ambassador Lindsay sashayed into the library where he spun Mona around into a chair and left the room, closing the door behind him.

"We meet again, Miss Moon." William Donovan stood by the fireplace, working on a neat bourbon.

Mona kept her composure. "Mr. Donovan, we have nothing more to say to each other."

"Was I right when I predicted that you would be contacted by the Swedes?"

"Why are you asking a question for which you already know the answer?"

"And?"

"Yes, I was contacted by a man by the name of Lars Dardel who claims to work for Ambassador Wollmar Boström."

"And?"

"I don't know if Dardel's claims are true. He may work for you, Mr. Donovan, and his contact was a setup to see how I would respond."

Donovan laughed. "That may be true. Now you are playing the Great Game."

"I don't want to play the Great Game. I am not another Mata Hari. I have enough stress in my life."

"Miss Moon, the Great Game is going to be forced upon you."

"We shall see." Mona rose for the door. "Don't contact me again, Mr. Donovan."

"One more question. Did he want copper ore?"

Refusing to reply, Mona sighed and opened the heavy carved panel door.

Just as she did, a woman's bloodcurdling scream tore through the ballroom and over the music gaily playing. People stopped dancing and looked about in confusion while the musicians stood up rubbernecking from their chairs. Guests began congregating in the hallway.

Both Mona and Donovan dashed out of the library toward the screaming and pushed their way through a crowd of bystanders. Mona saw a man lying face down in the cloakroom with blood trickling from the side of his mouth. His hair covered his face lying sideways on the floor. A woman stood over him still screaming. A waiter gently pulled the woman away, trying to calm her. Finally, her screaming stopped and just grunts and moans could be heard as the servant led the distraught woman into the ballroom where she was offered a chair.

Mona knelt and felt for a pulse. There was none.

Ambassador Lindsay pushed his way through the crowd. "Let me through, please. Stand back. Let me through. Please stand back everyone." Seeing the body, he asked Mona, "Can we help him?"

Mona shook her head. "He is beyond our help, sir. He's in God's hands now."

Lindsay crouched down and turned the body over.

It was Lars Dardel!

Mona searched for Donovan, but the man was nowhere to be found. She quickly stood up and scanned the crowd only to see Donovan discreetly leave the embassy through the kitchen. "Well, if that don't beat all!"

Alice sidled up next to Mona. "I guess the party's over. Let's go."

"We can't leave. This is a police matter now."

"You wanna bet? This ain't America, kid. This is British soil." Alice motioned to Maynard Pickard and bade good night to Ambassador Lindsay.

Before Mona, Alice, and Colonel Pickard escaped with the other guests rushing through the embassy kitchen, Lindsay grabbed Mona and took her aside. "Miss Moon, I'd advise you to be very careful. There are many dangerous people in Washington and the fact that Lars Dardel spoke to you before his death puts you in a precarious position. Beware and don't trust anyone, and I mean anyone!"

Lindsay didn't have to tell Mona that. She already knew!

5

Mona was poring over the morning paper when Violet announced, "Miss Mona, there is someone to see you."

"Who is it?"

Violet handed Mona a card. "He said he is here on instructions from President Roosevelt."

Mona studied the card. On it was printed the name of Abraham Scott with a phone number. No logo, company name, address, title, or position. Mona turned the card over. Nothing was on the back either. "Ask him to wait while I dress. I don't think it is appropriate to receive him in my negligee."

"Yes, miss," Violet said, giving a little giggle.

Mona rushed to change into a long sleeved navy dress, pleated at the waist and accentuated with a navy belt, and embellished by a white Peter Pan collar and cuffs. She put on navy pumps and pearl earrings. Looking in the mirror, Mona brushed her hair back and put on red lipstick, thinking she looked like the average Washington hausfrau.

Taking a deep breath, she entered the suite's living room where Abraham Scott sat, casually flipping his felt hat in his hands. "Mr. Scott. I am Mona Moon."

Scott stood. "Miss Moon. It looks like I have interrupted your breakfast, but I thought you'd be free. It's so seldom one eats breakfast at eleven."

"Do I hear a small reproach in your voice, Mr. Scott?"

Scott grinned. "I guess you do. I had my breakfast at seven this morning."

"Then you must be starving. Come and join me. I'd like to finish my breakfast before it gets stone cold."

"Be glad to."

Mona escorted Scott to the balcony where she had been enjoying her meal. "Please help your-self."

Mr. Hammond, the suite's butler, laid down

an extra plate and filled a water glass. Soon after, he put a glass of orange juice next to Mr. Scott. "May I serve you, sir?"

"Yes, please. Anything but pork."

Mr. Hammond filled Scott's plate with scrambled eggs, toast slathered with butter, pastries, and fruit.

"Thank you, Mr. Hammond. You may leave now."

"Very good, miss."

Mona dived into her eggs after putting strawberry jam on her toast. "I'm famished."

Scott glanced at Mona's hair, but said nothing.

Catching Scott's curious gaze, Mona said, "A strain of albinism runs in the Moon family."

"I don't quite grasp your meaning."

"You're wondering if my hair is dyed. It's natural. I have an aunt with hair almost the same color and my father had platinum hair."

"I apologize. I didn't mean to be so boorish."

"I'm used to it."

Scott laughed. "That people are boorish or the inquiries about your hair?"

Mona smiled. "Both I guess."

"Well, you don't mince words."

"Why should I?"

"I guess the very rich can say whatever they want."

Mona's eyes narrowed. "I was thinking along gender terms. Men say whatever they want, but they expect women always to be nice regardless of the truth. Even very rich women. I don't like that game. Speaking of games, Mr. Scott, who are you and what do you want?"

"Again I will apologize for my boorishness, especially if you pass me the strawberry jam."

Mona relaxed and handed Scott the jam. "You told Miss Tate that you were sent by President Roosevelt. Why should I believe that when your card contains no information other than a name? You could be some flimflam man working to rob me."

Between bites, Scott said, "You're quite right, Miss Moon. You should be suspicious."

Mona handed over a basket of fresh pastries to Scott. "Here, have some more of these. You need to eat up."

"My mother always complained that I was too thin. Said that it put her in a bad light and had the neighbors thinking that she didn't feed me."

Mona noticed that Scott ate in the European fashion of holding a fork and a knife throughout eating. Americans use one utensil at a time. "Was she a good cook?"

Scott wiped his mouth with the napkin. "The absolute worst. I shudder thinking about her cooking even today."

Mona laughed. Although mysterious and possibly dangerous, Scott was entertaining. He had warm brown eyes and dark hair slicked back with pomade. She didn't smell cigarette smoke on him, so Mr. Scott did not use tobacco. There was an eyeglass case in his jacket handkerchief pocket, which indicated Mr. Scott was nearsighted. His gray suit was several years old, but cut from the best wool material and his blue and gray tie was silk. Mona concluded Mr. Scott had seen better days in which to purchase the suit and tie, but had fallen economically the past year as the cuffs of his fresh white shirt were closed with buttons instead of cuff links. In regards to clothing for men, shirts were the first item needing to be replaced. Mona wanted to get a good look at Scott's shoes to see if there had been recent repairs, but resisted the temptation to peek under the table.

Scott looked about for Mr. Hammond. "May I have a glass of milk for these apple pastries?"

Mona asked Violet, who was standing nearby, to get a pitcher of milk.

Violet went off to find Mr. Hammond.

As soon as Violet was out of earshot, Mona said, "Okay, Mr. Scott, we are alone now. Who are you and what do you want?"

"I do work for President Roosevelt, but unofficially, of course."

Mona rolled her eyes. "Of course. Do you have anything to prove this?"

"I see by the morning newspaper scattered about, you were looking for an article about last night's debacle at the British Embassy. You won't find it."

"The afternoon paper then?"

"Never. The murder of Lars Dardel will never be mentioned in any newspaper. In fact, there will be no record of the event mentioned at all. Officially, Lars Dardel died peacefully in his bed last night from heart congestion."

Flabbergasted, Mona leaned back in her chair. "There seem to be an awful lot of murders going unreported in Washington."

"You're referring to the death of the German diplomat yesterday near your accommodations on the second floor of this hotel."

"You are very well informed, Mr. Scott. Are you here to blackmail me by associating the Moon name with these two murders?"

"No, miss. I am to be your liaison for William Donovan."

"Utterly outrageous!" Mona said, standing up and throwing her napkin on the table. "I will not be coerced, cornered, or corralled by a bunch of chest-pounding men. You tell your boss, he can go to the Devil."

Scott calmly slathered jam on his toast. "Please sit down, Miss Moon. I am here to tell you that your life and the life of Lord Farley are in danger."

Mona sat down. "What did you say?"

Scott took a bite of his toast. "Delicious jam. I must say the Willard does it right."

"Mr. Scott, I'm waiting."

"Countries do not plan in years. They plan in decades. Mostly multiple decades. Even the United States. And what the United States sees is that Adolf Hitler will become president and will ignore the Versailles Treaty by rebuilding the German military, thus letting it loose upon the world."

"I doubt that, Mr. Scott. Germany's economy is in tatters, and there is political infighting in the Reichstag."

Scott said, "You think Adolph Hitler is a blowhard."

"Don't you?"

"No, I believe the man is perfectly serious and when things go wrong as they always do, he is going to strike out at his scapegoats. You've heard his speeches. It's not just the Jews he's after but anyone or anything he deems unsuitable—Jehovah's Witnesses, Eastern Europeans, political opponents, unions, newspapers—groups that might oppose him. The man is dangerous."

Mona said, "People like him because he is charismatic, and he has a strong economic plan. You've got to admit he is a great orator. On the other hand, Hitler's ideology is unpleasant, that's for sure, and his association with Mussolini is cause for concern, but he has nothing to do with me."

"You can disagree with me on Hitler's personality all you like, but one thing is for real. Germany wants minerals. Without copper, iron, tin, they cannot rebuild their military, and they will get their minerals by hook or by crook. You own the largest copper mines in the northern hemisphere. You have already been contacted by Lars Dardel, a Swedish diplomat working as a German agent."

"Do you think he was killed because he contacted me?"

"I would like for you to tell me the entire conversation."

"There's not much to tell. He did ask about copper and if Moon Enterprises would sell to Sweden. I said I would consider it if the Swedish government contacted me. I made it clear I would not sell to a private individual."

"Under no circumstances must you sell to any country in Europe."

"We already have several contracts in Europe."

"You will need to cancel them."

Mona took a deep breath. She disliked being dictated to. She and her lawyer, Dexter Deatherage, had made a five year plan, and the U.S.

government seemed bent on tearing it to shreds.

Just at that moment, Violet brought in a pitcher of milk and set it on the table.

"Thank you, fair lady," Scott said, pouring the milk into his now empty water glass.

"Violet, please make sure that Mr. Scott and I are not disturbed."

Giving a forbidding look at Scott, Violet closed the French doors to the balcony and waited in the parlor.

"You were saying that Lord Farley and I are in danger, Mr. Scott."

"There are several of us who work incognito for the government, and our job is to strategize. We sort of play mental chess—like 'what might the other guy do if Moon Enterprises won't play ball with selling copper ore.' Well, I tell you what I'd do, Miss Moon. I'd bump you off, have your Aunt Melanie instated to Moon Enterprises as president, and get a board of toadies to do what she wanted. Then I would bribe or blackmail Melanie Moon to do as I ordered."

Mona did not show surprise that Scott knew who her aunt was and understood the woman's weak character. "Do you have proof of this plan?"

"Two German agents have been killed in twenty-four hours that have had some proximity to your person. The first man carried documents that have led us to believe the Nazis are planning to rearm. The second man was killed after he spoke to you about purchasing copper, which is needed to rearm. The world is playing a deadly game, and it has led to your doorstep. We feel that you will be contacted again, and if you refuse to sell the copper, you will be eliminated."

"Did you kill Lars Dardel?"

"I did not."

"Did a British agent kill Dardel?"

"We don't know for sure, but we think Dardel was killed because he made some error."

"Which was?"

"Not getting you to agree."

"Who was the woman screaming?"

"His wife. Emma Dardel. She found his body."

Mona thought that explained the initials on Dardel's cigarette case. "What does the Swedish government say?"

"They have kept mum. No official statement yet. Remember that the Swedes have claimed neutrality, but they lean pro-Germany."

"I'm quite flummoxed, Mr. Scott. Your story is fantastic."

"And yet, here I sit, having breakfast at lunchtime with the fabulous Miss Moon, spinning my tale."

Mona said, "What about Lord Farley? You said he was in danger, too."

"Lord Farley's father is on his deathbed if he hasn't already died while we were having breakfast. His lordship received a cable this morning to come to England at once. He will call you to tell you that your trip is off as he must hasten to his father's side. We believe Lord Farley will be contacted on his sea voyage by enemy agents."

"For what reason and by whom?"

Scott explained, "We know that the Prince of Wales is pro-German. After all, the Windsor family is really German, aren't they? Remember Kaiser Wilhelm was Queen Victoria's grandson. So, it is only natural that Germany wants pro-German MP's sitting in the House of Lords as well. Lord Farley will naturally take his father's position in the House of Lords. Just follow the natural conclusion."

"Lord Farley is fanatically anti-fascist. He will never be turned."

"And that is what will put his life in danger." Scott folded his napkin and took a last sip of milk. "Keep my card. Call that number whenever you want to see me. A woman will answer. She will hang up after twenty seconds, so keep your message short."

"I won't be calling, Mr. Scott, because I don't believe you."

Scott gave a nasty little smirk. "I wish you were correct, Miss Moon. It does sound like the stuff of second-rate spy novels, but I assure you I am right as you will soon see." He rose and gave a polite bow. "One last word, keep that snub nose revolver of yours close. You're gonna need it."

Surprised, Mona's mouth dropped open. She closed it quickly. Mona rapidly assessed that either the suite's maid or the butler, Mr. Hammond, had gone through her things.

Mona rang a small bell and Violet opened the French doors, whereupon, she ordered Violet to escort Mr. Scott to the hallway and lock the suite's door after him.

Pacing in the drawing room, Mona couldn't decide whether to tell Violet of the conversation with Scott or send her home on the next train. If Scott was correct, Mona should remove Violet from danger as soon as possible.

All of a sudden a ringing phone pulled Mona out of her deep contemplation.

Violet answered.

"Miss Mona, it's Lord Farley."

Mona's heart froze.

6

After a lengthy conversation, Mona put the phone receiver back into its cradle.

"Bad news, Miss Mona?" Violet asked.

Mona sat in a chair by the window and stared at the world humming outside.

"Miss Mona? May I do anything for you?"

"It seems our trip to England has been postponed. Lord Farley's father is ill. Very ill. Lord Farley is going on the next available boat and does not wish us to accompany him. He feels his father is dying, and this would not be an opportune time to visit."

"Surely, you can understand. Everything will be topsy turvy. It is only natural he would want to sort things out before you came."

Mona nodded. "I do. I certainly do, Violet.

It's just that we waited too long for me to meet his father. We wanted it to be perfect, but neither life nor death waits for perfect opportunities. I really should be by Robert's side and helping. He shouldn't be on his own facing this." Mona didn't voice that she was worried Robert would start drinking again.

"Lady Alice and her husband, Mr. Nithercott will be only a phone call away if Lord Farley needs help."

"I feel I should be with Robert."

Violet got a look of rapture on her face. "If his father dies, then Lord Farley will become duke. Just think of it—you will be a duchess."

"Robert's father dying changes everything for Robert and myself."

Violet's face fell. "Does it? In what way?"

"There will be great pressure for Lord Farley to marry one from his own class. I am just a commoner and an American at that."

"You are richer than any of those folks," Violet said indignantly.

"That doesn't matter to the British. They put more emphasis on titles and lineage. Oh, they like money and they might welcome mine, but it might not be enough for me to marry someone in Lord Farley's position." Mona rose from her seat. She was agitated and wanted to smash something. "Let's not think about that, Violet."

"Shall I start packing for home?"

"Not yet. I have some unfinished business left to do." Mona needed to see Alice Roosevelt, but hesitated going out by herself. She did not want to be approached by another agent and felt she would be targeted if alone. Mona got the weird feeling she was being spied upon. "When do the lads get here?"

"The Pinkertons and Samuel with Jamison shall be arriving this afternoon on the three o'clock train. Rupert Hunt will be at the hotel by eleven tonight. I got his telegram this morning."

"Any word from Dexter Deatherage?"

"Nothing as of yet."

"Then he hasn't heard about Robert's father. That's good. It hasn't hit the papers yet."

"What shall we do then?"

"Well, I feel discombobulated and strange. Let's go to the dining area and get something to eat. When a woman can't break, smash, or shoot something, the next best thing is to eat something sweet and have a nice cup of tea. I understand the Willard's cinnamon bread pudding is awfully good."

Violet looked at her wrist watch. "Then what?"

"I think we should stay in our rooms until the gentlemen arrive."

"Is there something going on, Miss Mona? You seem awfully skittish since Mr. Scott visited. Did he say something to you unbecoming?"

"No, Violet," Mona lied. She did not want to involve Violet unless it was absolutely necessary. "I'm just upset about our trip being canceled. I'm worried about Robert."

Violet bit her lip. It never occurred to her that the Duke's death could cause a break between Miss Mona and Lord Farley. She had just assumed that once the grieving period was over, they would get on with the marriage. It all seemed so complicated now. She wanted to hug Mona, but knew her employer was not the hugging sort. What could she do to make Mona feel better?

Mona followed Violet out of the suite and to the main floor by way of the stairs. "Wait a minute, Violet. I want to send a cable to Mr.

Deatherage. Please go ahead and order for me."

"All right." Violet headed into the dining room.

Mona approached the front desk and rang the bell.

A clerk stopped putting letters and telegrams into guest room key slots. "Yes, miss?"

"I'd like to send a telegram, please," Mona said, scribbling on the Western Union form. "I'd like it to go out now."

"We can accommodate."

Mona handed the paper to the clerk. As the hotel clerk read it, he turned pale. "Are you sure you want to send this, miss?"

"Word for word. Just as I wrote it."

IF I SHOULD DIE, NOT A NATURAL DEATH STOP INVESTIGATE STOP UNDER NO CIRCUMSTANCES LET AUNT MELANIE TAKE OVER STOP SEND CODED REPLY STOP

7

Samuel and the others arrived at the hotel around four o'clock. Mona rented out the entire west side of her floor. The Pinkertons were housed in their own suite directly across from Mona. Samuel and Jamison took over the butler and maid's room at the very end of the hallway, as Mona knew they would appreciate their own private rooms. She told her staff very little except that she was being hounded by men, who wanted her to sign foreign copper contracts, and she needed relief from their unwanted attentions. When Samuel broached the subject of Mona's trip to Great Britain, Mona replied that the trip had been temporarily pushed back.

Mona made it clear that one Pinkerton was to be stationed in the hallway at all times. The maid and Mr. Hammond, the butler, were excused as Samuel and Violet would tend to her personal needs. Each person was to get everything they needed like extra towels before taking possession of their suites as there would be no further room service. None of the hotel staff would be permitted in their rooms.

Of the six men, three men were to remain on the hotel floor at all times. Mona instructed them not to give anyone her whereabouts or any information about Moon Manor or Moon Enterprises. Idle talk would be cause for dismissal.

Jamison was told to rent two cars suitable for four people each and to check them for listening and explosive devices each time before they were driven.

Samuel and Jamison glanced at each other. They knew something was up as Mona did not like security details following her. In fact, she loathed them. So, what was the matter? Bombs! Jamison was not sure he would recognize such a thing off hand. He had no idea what a bomb looked like, but he knew every part that belonged in a car. If something looked out of place, he would spot it.

Violet stood behind Mona while she was giving instructions. She nervously wrung her handkerchief and nibbled her bottom lip. She realized Mona was not telling her everything. It both irritated and stimulated her. She wanted to be a bigger help to Mona, and she wanted something of excitement for herself. After all, she was ready to start living her life. There had to be something more than mending Miss Mona's clothes, and fetching tea. She wanted a grand adventure, but also to remain safe at the same time. Somehow, Violet felt that was not how life worked, so she was rattled when Mona began giving restrictive instructions to her staff. Violet felt strongly that it had very little to do with Lord Farley canceling their trip. Something else was not right, and she could see some mild anxiety on Samuel's and Jamison's faces. They felt it, too.

Mona said people were hounding her for copper contracts, but she didn't state who they were. Moon Enterprises was in the business of selling copper. Mr. Deatherage, Mona's lawyer, said traveling was always healthy for making new business contacts. It would seem that Mona would welcome inquiries for the Moon copper. It didn't make sense. Violet felt sure that Mona's unease had to do with the visits from the two G-men and Mr. Scott.

As soon as the men retired to their rooms, Mona ordered a mess of sandwiches, coffee, soda pops, and desserts for them. She knew Samuel had an enthusiasm for Coca-Cola and ordered him several cases. She and Violet would dine alone in their suite and stay in for the night.

Around midnight, Mona got a call from the front desk stating that a man named Rupert Hunt wished to come to her room. Having gone to bed already, Mona threw on some slacks and a shirt and met Hunt in the main lobby.

Violet donned a house dress and surreptitiously followed Mona. She saw Mona and Rupert Hunt go outside and across the street, talking for a few moments. Violet didn't know exactly what Hunt did for Moon Enterprises, but knew that he posed as an assistant professor to get Mona on an expedition to Eastern Kentucky. She had heard Lord Farley and Mona arguing when she hired Hunt to act as her eyes and ears at her mines in the West. Lord Farley said Hunt was a little weasel who almost got them killed. Mona said his nefarious skills might prove to be invaluable to her.

Now Hunt was here in Washington getting instructions from Miss Mona. Violet clutched at the collar of her house gown. She couldn't help thinking that Mona was not candid about the last two days, and somehow she was in danger. Oh, how she wished Lord Farley was here. He would confront Mona for the truth.

Violet wouldn't dare!

8

While she and Violet were having breakfast in the dining room, a hotel clerk handed Mona an ivory envelope made of expensive paper. It was addressed to her with elaborate calligraphy.

The clerk informed Mona, "Miss Moon, there's a British Embassy footman outside waiting for your response."

Mona asked the clerk to wait while she read the enclosed note.

"Who's it from?" Violet asked, trying to read the return address.

"It's from Lady Lindsay. She wants me to come to lunch this afternoon."

"Are you going?"

"I think I shall."

As if anticipating Mona's next move, the clerk

handed Mona a blank envelope with crisp stationery with the Willard's letterhead.

Mona scribbled on the stationary and inserted it into the envelope. After writing Lady Lindsay's name on the front of the envelope, she handed it back to the clerk. "Please tell the footman to deliver this personally to Lady Lindsay."

"Very good, miss." He went off in search of the footman.

Mona continued to eat her poached eggs in silence.

"Shall I accompany you?" Violet so wanted to see the British Embassy.

"I have a task for you while I'm with Lady Lindsay. Are you game?"

Violet was disappointed, but tried not to show it.

Mona curbed her smile when she noticed Violet's fallen expression. "What I am asking you to do might be construed as naughty but not dangerous."

"Really? How naughty?"

"I want you to go to the maid's section in the basement on the pretense of looking for a sewing machine to mend a dress. Once there I want you to ask about a German who had a room near us on the second floor."

"What kind of things?"

"Like his name for starters. Anything you can find out about him. Was he a good tipper? How often did he check into the Willard? Was there anything unusual about his habits or clothing? Anything at all about the man." Mona looked at Violet's bright eyes. "Will you do it?"

"I think I can, but what if the maids don't want to talk?"

"I will give you six five dollar bills. That might loosen some tongues, but remember to be discreet. Don't go down there with both barrels blazing. A whisper here. A whisper there."

"What if they don't spill?"

"Ask the bell boys. Flirt. Men always open up when a pretty girl smiles at them."

Violet blushed. "You think I'm pretty."

"I think that when you are thirty, you are going to be devastating. Right now, you are just starting to bloom."

Violet put her hand to her cheek, feeling the heat rise. "Bless you for that, Miss Mona."

"But what's more important, Violet, is that you are intelligent and have a kind heart. Nice looks can only get you so far." Mona looked at her watch. "Oh, goodness, I'm late. Jamison is waiting for me."

"You're leaving?"

"I'm going to make a stop before I head out to the British Embassy. You go on back to the room. The five-dollar bills are on my dressing room table."

"Where are you going?"

"I have to make a pit stop at a bank first. We are running out of cash."

"The Willard will let you run a tab."

"Not for what I need. Only cash will do. Gotta run. Good luck to you." Mona rose and headed to the main lobby.

One of two Pinkertons who had been breakfasting at another table got up and followed her out.

The other security man escorted Violet back up to her suite, which he checked before he let Violet inside.

Violet hurried to Mona's bedroom and found the bills. Stuffing them inside her dress hip pocket, she tore a seam in one of Mona's expensive evening gowns.

Now she was ready.

9

"Good afternoon, Lady Lindsay," Mona said, after being shown into a conservatory.

"So nice to see you again, Miss Moon," Lady Lindsay said, extending her hand.

Mona shook it in a perfunctory manner. She certainly was not going to kiss it. "It is very kind of you to invite me so soon after the embassy ball."

"You mentioned my rose garden and I thought you might want to see the new one I planted at the embassy. I thought we might stroll through it before I ring for lunch."

Mona said, "That would be delightful."

Since Lady Lindsay was so stiff and formal, Mona wondered about the purpose of the lunch invitation. She doubted that Lady Lindsay really wanted to show off her rose garden.

"Let's go through here," Lady Lindsay said, showing the way out of the conservatory and into a red brick-walled garden space at the back of the embassy.

Mona marveled at the variety of plants and the variation of color.

"Do you garden, Miss Moon?"

"I told you that I dabbled in it. I did try your rose garden plan on my own, but it failed."

"I believed that I said that you might have possibly used the wrong manure."

"Yes, I remembered you said that."

Lady Lindsay pursed her lips. "I thought you might. I must apologize for my rudeness. I wasn't really speaking of manure in that sense."

Mona faced Lady Lindsay. "I got the true meaning of your statement, Lady Lindsay. I am used to boors trying to make jokes at my expense, but I always manage to get the last laugh."

Lady Lindsay seemed a little startled. "Well, you do speak your mind."

"As do you."

"Then let's not waste each other's time."

"Sounds good to me."

Lady Lindsay pointed to a pair of glistening, black wrought iron chairs sitting on a circular patio. "Let's sit, shall we?"

Mona sat. Upon that point Lady Lindsay offered her a cigarette. "I don't smoke."

"They *are* wretched things. The stench on a person's clothes and hair is almost unpalatable."

"Then why smoke?"

"Nervous habit, I suppose," Lady Lindsay said, lighting up. She reached for an ashtray sitting on a nearby table. Lindsay pondered for a moment before speaking. "I'm an American, you know."

Mona nodded.

"Ronald's first wife was Martha, my cousin. We are both grandnieces of General William Tecumseh Sherman."

"I've heard."

"Do you think that odd? I mean being married to two women of the same family."

"I don't consider it at all. I have other things to occupy my mind."

Lindsay scrutinized Mona. "You're a tough cookie. People are usually impressed by that fact."

"I'll take that as a compliment."

"You are from New York?"

Mona said, "But my family is Southern. Those below the Mason-Dixon line might have negative feelings toward anyone related to General Sherman, who burned his way through the countryside to the Atlantic Ocean."

Lady Lindsay inhaled deeply on the cigarette. "Are you one of those people, Miss Moon?"

"I think it best not to converse about the Civil War. Tempers still flare discussing old grudges. I want to look toward the future. I say let the dead bury the dead."

"I have been told that you were a cartographer and worked in Mesopotamia."

"Yes, I am a great admirer of Gertrude Bell. I have studied all the great explorers like Richard Burton and T. E. Lawrence and read all their works."

Lady Lindsay asked, "Did you ever meet Gertrude Bell?"

"Miss Bell had been long gone before I worked in Mesopotamia."

"Miss Bell is an example of what British ingenuity can do for the world. I know her family quite well."

"While I admire Miss Bell's work, I feel her borders for the countries carved out of Mesopotamia will cause a great deal of harm."

"In what way?"

"The same way religion has divided the Catholics and the Protestants in Ireland. The Sunni and Shiite Muslims will never live in harmony. And then there are the Kurds."

"The British will keep the peace." Lady Lindsay's eyes lit up. "Let's talk about the future."

"What about it?" Mona asked, growing tired of this cat and mouse conversation.

"Great Britain is the leader of the Western world."

"I think there are some who would disagree with that, but go on."

"It is important to Europe and even to the United States that Great Britain maintains its present position, but it can't do that without minerals."

"I'm listening." Mona waved smoke away.

"At the moment, the sun never sets on the British Empire, but the truth of the matter is that Great Britain is a broken country. Oh, you can't see the rot firsthand, but the Great War and now this blasted Depression have compromised Great Britain to such a degree that maybe in thirty years or less, there will be no British Empire. It will cease to exist."

"Is that such a bad thing, Lady Lindsay? The British Empire has brought a great deal of misery to a great many people."

"I don't deny we have made mistakes, but we have brought law where there was none and established educational and medical institutions. You can't deny the British have improved the standard of living wherever we have been."

Mona didn't reply at first. There was truth in what Lady Lindsay said. It was also true Great Britain had bled India economically dry, but she simply didn't want to make an enemy of this woman who held immense influence in Washington.

Irritated at Mona's silence, Lady Lindsay said, "Let me put it this way. Would you rather see Great Britain have your copper or Germany?"

"So you are pitching on behalf of the British government. I just had someone tell me not to sell to Europe at all."

"Surely you can see from the newspapers that

democracy in Europe is threatened, and if we go down, Miss Moon, the United States is next."

"I think Europe should mind its own business, and America should do the same."

Lady Lindsay looked surprised and snubbed out her cigarette. "I didn't realize that you were an isolationist, Miss Moon. I pictured you more as a citizen of the world since you are going to marry Lord Farley. Surely, you must have sympathy for the country of his birth."

"At the moment, I have no contracts with Great Britain, but I will entertain the idea for information. I'd like to see the security report on Lars Dardel and the coroner's report on his death. I'm sure one of your people did the autopsy. I don't even know how he died."

"Dardel was stabbed to death."

"With what?"

"A small knife perhaps, but *our* entire cutlery was accounted for. Whoever killed Dardel brought the weapon with him."

"Any idea who did it?"

Lady Lindsay shook her head. "It could have been a half dozen people at the party. Washington is crawling with secret agents, spies, and provocateurs, and most of them have diplomatic status."

"Dardel was a low-level diplomat. Why was he invited to the party?"

"You would have to ask my husband. I didn't make the guest list. I never do."

"Why were you so resentful of me coming to the ball?"

"Oh please, must we go into that? I was wrong. I admit it."

"I hold the keys to the copper. Belly up to the bar, so to speak."

Lady Lindsay hesitated and then decided to come clean. "It was because Alice Longworth bullied my husband for an invitation on your behalf."

"Your husband didn't seem to mind my being at the ball. That doesn't explain your rudeness."

Lady Lindsay said, "I did apologize for that. I assumed you made Alice get that invitation for you. I considered you an upstart. A social climber."

"You're wrong about Alice getting me that invitation. It was a personal request from Lord Farley to your husband."

Realizing her mistake, Lady Lindsay gasped. "I do, indeed, apologize. It seems I have been a frightful beast. Ronald is going to be so cross with me if he finds out what I've said."

"I would hate for him to find out." Mona stared hard at Lady Lindsay. "Will you get that report for me?"

"A report wasn't done."

"The British make a record of every time they pass wind. I know this incident was reported to MI6 that very night."

"There's no need to be crude, Miss Moon. You won't make friends that way."

Mona smirked. "You know what they say in this town—if you want a friend in Washington, get a dog."

10

Violet headed down to the warren of offices and workspaces hidden in the basement of the Willard. Staffers were scurrying about amongst the clatter of deliveries, whooshing sounds of new electric washing machines, and shouts of supervisors ordering their employees about.

A harried-looking woman wearing her hair in a severe bun and a pinched nose stopped Violet before she ventured far. "I am Mrs. Ruttle. May I help you, young lady?"

"Yes, yes," Violet stammered. She held out Mona's dress. "I need a sewing machine to mend my mistress' dress, please."

"We have several seamstresses who can help you. How bad is the rip?"

Violet clutched the dress tightly against her

waist. "Thank you, but I prefer to do it myself. My mistress doesn't like anyone handling her clothes but me."

The woman looked Violet up and down before snapping her fingers at one of the maids loading up her cart. "Hilda, come here."

"Yes, Mrs. Ruttle?"

"Take this young woman to the sewing division and show her a machine." Hilda looked curiously at Violet. "Yes, ma'am."

"Thank you," Violet said.

"As soon as you finish, young woman, you should leave this area immediately. Guests are not permitted at this level of the hotel. Understand?"

"Yes, ma'am, and thank you again."

Mrs. Ruttle looked Violet up and down again sizing her up. Pleased at Violet's politeness, she waved the two young girls away and went about her business.

Since Hilda was near her own age, Violet felt emboldened to speak. "Is she your boss?"

Hilda nodded while walking swiftly down a green painted corridor.

"Is she a good boss?"

"Why would you want to know that, miss?"

Violet shrugged. "We both work for women. I was just making conversation. It's lonely sometimes, you know? I don't know anyone here my own age."

Hilda's eyes softened. "Sorry, miss. The staff has to be careful talking to the guests. We can be fired for any minor indiscretion."

Ah oh. Violet's heart sank. How was she going to get any information now?

Hilda offered, "Yes, Mrs. Ruttle is a good boss. A little rough sometimes, but very fair. She has girls from all over the country working for her—Irish, Polish, Slovenians, Jews, blacks, and she plays no favorites. Besides training us, she teaches us hygiene and helps us get our teeth fixed. You can't work at the Willard without smelling sweet and having a nice smile. Most girls work here for two years, get trained, and then hire out to posh homes."

Feeling a bit more confident, Violet blurted out, "I work for Mona Moon."

"The lady with the white hair?"

Violet nodded.

"I hear she rented out the entire fourth floor."

"Just the west side of the fourth floor."

"She must be awfully rich."

"One of the richest."

"What's she like?"

"She's like Mrs. Ruttle I suspect. Tough, but nice."

"I like bosses like that. You know where you stand."

Violet agreed. "Exactly."

Hilda stopped and opened a door. "Here we are." She showed Violet into a room where six sewing machines were neatly spaced out in a row against the back wall. Several were being used by seamstresses hired by the hotel. "You'll find the thread you need in the cupboard over there."

"Thank you."

"We girls need to stick together."

"Hey, wait a minute, I'm free after I finish this dress. How about I take you to lunch? I want to go to the Lincoln Memorial but I have no idea of how to get there."

Hilda's eyes brightened. "You would take me to tea?"

"Why not? A thank you for your kindness, especially if you join me for the Lincoln Memorial. I don't want to go by myself."

"I do have a nice hat I could wear." Hilda thought for a moment. "I get off at three. Can you wait until then?"

"A perfect time for tea!"

"I know a little place for us serving girls. Not too fancy, but respectable and clean. They serve the nicest little cakes."

"Sounds perfect. I'll wait for you out on the sidewalk in front of the hotel."

"Can you wait by the drugstore around the corner? I don't want to get into trouble with the management."

Violet winked. "I'll be there."

"See ya, then."

"Bye." Violet selected a machine and, working the floor pedals, sewed Mona's dress with black thread already spooled into the machine, all the while fervently hoping this contact with Hilda would work out. Otherwise an entire day would be wasted.

11

Samuel found a little kitchen in the butler's area used for private parties in the suites. He heated up fried chicken, mashed yams, and pickled green beans, which he paired with a white wine and sweet iced tea. He served Violet and Mona their evening meal on the balcony.

Mona tried the green beans and sat back in her chair astonished.

"What do you think, Miss Mona?" Samuel asked.

"I think these green beans might put your mama's to shame, Samuel. Now I know you didn't cook this meal from scratch. Fess up."

Samuel grinned. "Went for a walk today and found a neighborhood not too far from the hotel. Came across a little hole-in-the-wall place serving real down-home Southern vittles. I ate my full and then brought some back for you. Thought you and Miss Violet might be homesick for our kind of food."

"I hope you took a Pinkerton with you," Mona admonished.

"Don't worry, Miss Mona. I was careful. Went out the servants' entrance. Anybody watching would just think I was part of the hotel's staff finished with his shift."

"I know the security is stifling, but we need to be careful until we get home."

"When will that be, Miss Mona?"

"I don't know, Samuel. Maybe another week or more."

Samuel sighed. He didn't like Washington, D.C. It was too big of a city for him.

Excusing himself, an unhappy Samuel went to heat up supper for Jamison and himself.

The Pinkertons were left on their own to do as they pleased. Two of them went to the dining room while the others guarded the floor and waited their turn to eat.

Mona slathered a soft dinner roll with butter, which was a weakness. Mona loved the salty and cool taste of butter.

Violet watched in fascination. "Why don't you just eat a spoon of butter?"

Mona looked confused for a moment and then chuckled. "I do put it on a bit thick, don't I?" She wiped some of the butter off with her knife. "That's better."

"Everything in moderation, my mother always says."

"Your mother is correct, Violet. Remember that." Mona picked up a chicken wing with her fingers. "Let's forget about fancy manners tonight and eat like home folks."

"Yes, let's." Violet picked up a chicken leg and bit into it.

"Was your day productive?"

Violet wiped the chicken grease off her lips. "I think so, Miss Mona. I made friends with a maid. We had tea together and went to see the Lincoln Memorial. Have you visited it, Miss Mona? Oh, it is so grand. You've got to see it before we leave."

"Did you learn anything?"

"My friend, Hilda, told me a maid who worked on the second floor told her that a man was murdered several doors down from us. She told my friend that it was kept hush hush. The porters told this maid that the body was taken out the back way in a steamer trunk in the middle of the night."

"Did Hilda know the man's name?"

"Said he called himself Otto Mueller, but the maid saw a letter that had fallen from his pocket once when cleaning. When she picked it up off the floor, Mr. Mueller got upset and yelled at her. Before she left his room in tears, the maid noticed it was in care of the German Embassy and the name was different."

"Did the maid tell your friend the name on the letter?"

"No. Remember this is third-hand information."

"Anything else your friend told you?"

"Mr. Mueller came once a month like clockwork. He was middle-aged, paunchy, married, but took off his wedding ring when he came. The maid noticed a tan line on his ring finger."

"Nothing else? Even the smallest detail."

"He reeked of cheap cologne and his breath smelled badly. The maid figured that one of his teeth was rotten. I learned today that the maids put great store on nice looking teeth, so they would notice a bad mouth."

"That's interesting. Did he meet with anyone?"

"I don't know. I could ask Hilda but she didn't mention any visitors."

"Is that all?"

"Nothing else really, except Mr. Mueller liked jazz and would buy jazz records when in town."

Mona got up and picked up the phone receiver. "Concierge desk, please." She paused for a moment. "Hello. Is there a jazz club in town?" Mona picked up a pencil and wrote on a message tablet near the phone. "Whereabouts is that again?" She wrote some more. "Yes, thank you. No, I won't need a car. I have my own." Mona put down the receiver and turned to Violet.

"I hope you brought along an evening dress that's loose around the hips."

"I brought several. Why?"

"Cause we are going dancing!"

12

"Sorry, but I can't let you ladies in without an escort. We don't let in working girls," said the bouncer at the front door of the juke joint located in a dirty alleyway.

"You'd be horsewhipped for saying something nasty like that back home," Violet protested. She was simply aghast.

Mona said, "We may be working girls, but not the sort to which you are referring." She pushed by the bouncer who responded by grabbing her arm. Mona swirled on him in a fury.

"Hey, hey, now. Let's all be friends," said a calm voice. "Here, Fred. I know these ladies, and they are with me."

Mona looked up to see Rupert Hunt pry the bouncer's large hand from her wrist. As she rubbed her arm, Rupert put a ten dollar bill into the bouncer's right pocket.

Rupert said, "Thanks, Fred. I'll take it from here."

"My name's not Fred."

"Everyone is named Fred in a place like this," Rupert replied, before escorting the ladies to his table. "Sit here, please." Weaving a little on his feet, Rupert dusted off the chairs before pulling them out for Mona and Violet.

Concluding that Rupert was a little smashed, Mona asked, "How long have you been on this toot?"

"You wanted information, so I had to buy everyone lots of drinks and bribe several waiters, which brings up the fact I'm all out of money. Need more cash."

"What did I buy with this money?"

Rupert beckoned a waiter. "Pink champagne cocktail for the lady, and a Shirley Temple for the child."

"I'm old enough to have an alcoholic drink," Violet shouted over the loud talking in the club.

"She still gets a Shirley Temple," Rupert said. "I'll take a gin and tonic. Easy on the tonic."

When Violet started to protest, Rupert threatened, "Shut up if you know what's good for you." He gave Violet the once over. "You've grown up a bit since I last saw you."

"You mean the time when you kidnapped Miss Mona and spirited her away to Eastern Kentucky looking for that fake silver mine?"

"Miss Mona came willingly. No force was ever used."

"You tricked her and almost got her killed."

"Let's stay on point," Mona advised. She lit the candle on the table which sat in a darkened corner of the jazz club. "Now Violet, I want to teach you something about coming to places like this. First thing you do is look to see where the exits are in case of a fire or police raid."

Violet looked around frantically. "Oh, I don't like this place, Miss Mona. It's so dark, and it stinks like something sour."

"Yes, Miss Violet, what you smell is sin," Rupert teased.

"Second thing you do is never drink from an open glass. Order drinks from a bottle and have the waiter open the bottle in front of you. Got that?"

"Yes, miss."

"And never leave your drink unattended. If you dance, order a fresh bottle."

Rupert complained, "Geez, are you her mother?"

"Every young woman needs an older woman to teach her the underhanded tricks of that skunk on the prowl we call man."

"I believe the term is wolf."

"A wolf is too noble a creature. He attacks with no subterfuge. Skunk or rat is a better term."

"Somebody sure got your knickers in a knot."

Mona ignored Rupert and waited patiently for the waiter to serve the cocktails. After thanking him, she put the drinks aside and ordered two bottled beers.

Rupert blew out the candle. "And never light a candle when on a nefarious visit."

"I can barely see you, Rupert," Mona said.

"That's the point," Rupert replied. "Hey, gals. Laugh a little. Look like you're enjoying yourselves. People are watching."

Violet glanced around swiveling in her chair. "Who? Who's watching us?"

Irritated, Rupert asked Mona, "Why did you

bring the kid along?"

"Like Violet says, she's old enough. Needs to know things, but I'm taking it slow with her." Mona paused while the waiter served the beers.

Admonishing Violet, Rupert said, "Hey, don't look around like some redneck goober who just got to town."

"Who are you to address me so?" Violet demanded.

Rupert drew back in his chair. "Well, you've got some spunk, I must say, but be cool, little Violet."

The black musicians wandered back on stage and picked up their instruments. Since they drew everyone's attention, Rupert scooted closer to Mona and put his arm around her.

Mona drew closer and played along. Whispering in Rupert's ear, she asked, "Find anything?"

"Yeah, a man who called himself Otto Mueller visited this club many times over the past two years. He was a jazz enthusiast and quite knowledgeable about music. He sometimes played clarinet with the band after hours."

"Was he a German national?"

"I'm getting to that."

Mona played with Rupert's tie and smiled a lot. "Keep going."

"He had been having an affair with the band's lead singer for the past seven months."

"That would explain the line on his ring finger."

"Huh?"

"Never mind. Go on."

"The waiter told me that he was infatuated with her and was her sugar daddy, but only saw her once a month."

"Convenient."

"He was sometimes visited by a man with light hair and eyes. Youngish. Slim. They spoke German together, but I was told the younger man's accent was different. It would help if I had some photographs of these people."

"I couldn't finagle it. I don't think Otto Mueller was the man's real name." Mona took a sip of her beer. "See if the name of Lars Dardel is familiar around here."

"Will do."

At that moment, a beautiful black woman dressed in a shimmering gold dress with fringe stepped onto the stage.

"Is that the woman?"

Rupert nodded.

"Find out her address, will you?"

"Will do."

"See if she is up for another sugar daddy."

"My pleasure."

"One more thing, was this Otto Mueller a Nazi?"

Rupert stared at the black songstress looking at a sheet of music. "If he was, he wasn't a very dedicated one."

"We need to go. It's past Violet's bedtime."

Violet asked, "Oh, can't we stay and listen to the lady sing?"

"One song and then we're gone."

The woman went up to the microphone and sang a sad ballet of losing the man she loved, enthralling the audience.

Mona wondered if she was singing about Otto Mueller. Why had this beautiful woman been entangled with a fat, middle-aged German with bad teeth? Surely she could have done better.

Out of the corner of her eye, she saw Abraham Scott inching his way to an empty table on the far side of the room. Mona instinctively put her hand up to shield her face.

"What's the matter?" Rupert asked, noticing Mona's trepidation.

"That man on the other side, wearing a striped waist coat and gray suit."

Rupert casually shifted his chair and glanced over. "The man with the slick, dark hair and wearing glasses?"

"Yes."

"What about him?"

"He came to see me at the Willard. Said he was working for President Roosevelt."

Rupert lit a cigarette and offered Mona and Violet one. "What did he want?"

Mona waved the cigarette case away. "Said his name was Abraham Scott and wanted me to spy for the government."

Rupert shrugged and asked, "I'm impressed. What did you say?"

"Blew him off. Do you think he followed us here?"

"Could be, but seems like he's more interested in our little songbird."

"Check it out, will you?"

"I can't do this all by myself. You've got me

investigating three people now. I need more operatives. I can hire some local boys from Washington."

"All right. Tell them no more than you have to and certainly don't mention my name."

"No problem. Look, Scott has gone to the gents. Now's a good time for you to skedaddle."

Mona opened her purse and slipped Rupert an envelope with a large amount of cash under the table. "Call me tonight, no matter how late. I want a report at least several times a day."

"It's your funeral."

Mona left the table with Violet trailing behind. Once outside, Mona signaled for Jamison to pull the car up. Samuel was with him.

Once inside the warmth and security of the car, Mona asked, "Tell me, gentlemen, why would a beautiful, talented black woman who has her own income be with an ugly white man twice her age."

Looking in the rearview mirror, Jamison replied, "The same reason a white girl would be, Miss Mona. Hard times require hard measures."

"Fair enough. It was a stupid question. Forgive me."

There was an uncomfortable silence on the way back to the hotel until Violet, who had learned quite a bit about life this night, wanted to learn more. She asked, "What's a sugar daddy?"

13

The car swerved a bit before Jamison got it under control. He seemed giddy with laughter.

Flustered, Samuel whipped his head around. "Where did you hear that term, young woman?"

"Tonight with Miss Mona. Is it bad?" She looked at Mona, who was laughing.

Mona patted Violet's shoulder, saying, "I'll explain when we get back to the hotel. I don't want to embarrass Jamison or Samuel."

"This is what you get for toting Miss Violet off to some honkytonk," Samuel said.

"It was a jazz club."

"Jazz is bordello music."

Surprised, Mona said, "Next you're going to say it's the Devil's tunes. I had no idea you were such a choir boy, Samuel."

Samuel made a face and turned around in the front seat.

Nothing more was said until they arrived at the Willard. Jamison and Samuel waited until the two women entered the hotel before they went to park the car.

Mona asked the desk clerk if there were any messages or telegrams for her. There were none.

Violet and Mona rode the elevator in silence while Mona took note of who got off on which floor. They were the only ones to ride to the fourth floor. As the elevator doors slid open, Mona knew instantly that something was wrong. There was no Pinkerton guarding the west wing.

Mona pushed Violet behind her and pulled out her gun. She banged at the first door on the right. When no one answered, she gingerly turned the doorknob and swung the door open. All four Pinkertons were passed out on the floor.

Suddenly, the stairwell door opened and Mona swung around with the gun.

"Whoa, it's us," Samuel said, looking pointedly at the gun.

"Where is everyone?" Jamison asked, carrying a greasy bag of glazed donuts.

Mona motioned to the Pinkertons' room. "Passed out it seems."

Jamison asked, "Sure they're not dead?"

"I see their chests moving," Samuel said, peering into the room.

"Go check your rooms," Mona ordered.

Samuel checked the servants' rooms, turning on all the lights with Mona following him. "Seems okay. Have you checked your suite?"

"Not yet. I didn't want to go into it without some backup."

"I'm your man."

"Let's go."

Samuel swung open Mona's suite door. He was half expecting someone to shoot at him. When nothing happened, he reached in and turned on the lights.

Mona stepped inside with her gun drawn.

Jamison drew up behind her. "Lordy, what a mess. I knew I should have brought my shotgun from home."

Mona's suite had been turned upside down and ravaged.

Violet peeped inside. "Oh!" she said, clamping her hand over her mouth.

"Wait out in the hallway with Jamison, Violet. Samuel and I will take care of this."

Samuel and Mona searched each room, peeking under the beds, in the wardrobes, balconies, and even the bathtubs. Satisfied that no one was still around, Mona put her gun away and plopped down on her bed. "Gee, they took all my silk stockings and even my extra garter belt."

"They must have a girlfriend," Samuel said, picking up pillows and scattered clothing.

"You said 'they.'"

"Surely one man didn't do this."

Almost in tears, Violet asked, "Shall I call for the house detective, Miss Mona?"

Mona shook her head. "Not now, but I'm having those Pinkertons replaced—the oafs." Seeing Violet so distressed, Mona went over and put her arms around the shaking girl. "Violet, I think you should go home on the next train. I wasn't expecting all this drama, and this is too much for you. I want you to be safe."

"I'm not crying because I'm frightened. I'm crying because my new polka-dotted church-going dress is ruined. They stepped on it and got it dirty. I'll never get that filth out."

"Well, don't clean the dress yet. It may be a clue. We'll deal with this mess in the morning, but tomorrow you are going back to Lexington. Samuel will escort you home."

Violet looked defiant. "No, Miss Mona. I will not. If Samuel and I return home, that leaves just you and Jamison—and those Pinkertons are no-accounts. You can have a hundred of those men on your payroll, and they still couldn't put the lid on the tooth powder tin between them."

Jamison spoke up, "Miss Violet is right. You need all three of us. At least, until we get more guards."

"What do you think, Samuel?"

"I think we should all pack up and go home. I know you won't because you are not telling us everything. We are working in the dark. Not nice, Miss Mona. Not nice to do to us, especially after this."

"I see I'm outvoted. Let's go to bed and deal with this in the morning. I'm exhausted and know you must be too."

"If that's the way you want to play this," Samuel said disapprovingly.

"It's the way I must play it. I'm sorry, but I

can't say more. At least at this time." Mona motioned to the hallway. "Lock the Pinkertons in their room."

"I think I should call a doctor for them," Samuel said.

"I think they were given a Mickey to make them sleep, but probably a good idea. The hotel should have a doctor on call. Can you take care of it?"

"Yes, miss. Now, you and Miss Violet go on to bed. I'll handle the Pinkertons."

"Thank you, Samuel. Thank you, Jamison. You both have been a big help."

Both men nodded and left, closing the suite's door behind them.

Violet ran over and locked the door. "Miss Mona?"

"Yes?"

"May I sleep with you tonight?"

Mona smiled. "Of course, you can. I was thinking company might help the rest of the night seem more peaceful." Mona looked out the window. "What's left of the night."

As Violet rushed off to change, Mona couldn't help but think she really wanted Robert with her. She needed to fall into his arms, smelling his woodsy cologne, the horse sweat on his tweed jacket, and his sweet breath after he chewed on peppermint. Oh, how she missed him. He would know whom to call and what to do. Why hadn't she heard from him?

It wasn't long before Violet hurried back into Mona's bedroom, locking the door.

She turned and shot Mona a beseeching look.

As though she knew exactly what Violet was thinking, Mona jumped up and ran over to the door. Without uttering a word to each other, Mona and Violet pushed a small bureau in front of the door.

Satisfied that no one could reach them while they slept, they still left the bathroom light on to illuminate the room. Exhausted from the tiring day, they both quickly fell asleep.

That's why they didn't hear the telephone ring and ring and ring in the suite's drawing room.

Somebody was desperately trying to get hold of Mona to inform her that Lawrence Robert Emerton Dagobert Farley's father had died, and Robert was now Duke of Brynelleth.

God save the King!

14

Mona learned the next day that the Pinkerton men had been sedated via their dinners or the wine ordered from the Willard main kitchen. The hotel manager was apoplectic when he saw the state of Mona's suite, but could not give any answers as to the identity of the culprits, how the sedative got into their food, or who even delivered the room service orders.

Although he apologized profusely, it was evident he wanted Mona and her entourage to leave. He couldn't handle any more crises at the hotel as his nerves were being pushed beyond their limits. Even in Washington, this amount of higgledy-piggledy mischief was unusual.

Seeing that the manager was not going to help further, Mona dismissed him and pulled out a business card from her purse. Dialing the number on the card, she said, "Tell Scott I want to see him," and hung up.

Overhearing the abrupt message, Violet asked, "Why do you want him, Miss Moon?"

"I want to see if he had anything to do with this. He could be putting pressure on me, Violet."

"Then let's go home and let Mr. Deatherage handle this."

"These men would just follow me to Lexington and try every trick in the book to have access to my copper. They would ruin you, me, Mr. Thomas, our friends, Lord Farley—anyone we know and love to put pressure on me. I need to stop this here and now."

"I wish you'd tell me what is going on. Jamison, Samuel, and I are working in the dark. Everything has us frantic. It's not right to send us out on tasks for you when we don't even know if we are in danger."

Before Mona could respond, there was a knock and the door opened. Abraham Scott walked in with hat in hands flipping it nonchalantly, looking about the torn up suite. He whistled and said, "Boy, oh, boy, they did a number on you. Look at this mess."

Mona bristled. "How did you get here so fast? I just called."

Scott snickered. "I knew about this last night."

"Really?"

Violet clutched Mona's arm. "Who is this man really?"

"He's an agent working for President Roosevelt."

Scott looked disgruntled. "You shouldn't have told the little girl that, Miss Mona. We had a deal."

"Actually, we didn't." Mona moved some ripped up sofa pillows and sat down. She motioned for Scott to sit down as well.

He chose an armchair that had been cut apart and the stuffing pulled out. "Does she have to be here?" he asked, staring at Violet.

Violet defiantly moved behind Mona's chair.

"I would like for her to stay." Before Scott could reply, Mona asked, "How did you know about this last night?"

"My man saw the men who did it."

"You sure it wasn't your men or even you?"

"Why point the finger at me?"

"I think you are creating chaos to reel me in."

He twisted his lips, saying, "My men didn't do this."

"Who was it?"

"Ambassador Lindsay's lads." He studied Mona to see her reaction to the news.

Mona didn't blink.

"Now, what I can't figure out is why Ambassador Lindsay would search your apartment at the Willard and cause so much damage. This type of thing is usually done with a little bit more finesse."

Mona stood. "Thank you for coming, Mr. Scott. You gave me the information I needed."

Scott grinned and rose from his chair. "I get it. You only wanted to know who did this."

"I am grateful you were honest with me."

"How can you tell? I could be lying."

"I usually know when men are lying. Tell me, Mr. Scott, do you like jazz?"

Scott drew back. "How did you know?"

"I saw you last night at the club."

Scott whistled again. "You sure do get around, Miss Mona. I didn't even see you. I take it you were there."

"The German agent who was killed by your man was also a jazz enthusiast. I know that he and the lovely nightingale were intimate friends. Are you intimate friends with the nightingale as well, Mr. Scott?" Mona took a chance and lied, "I saw you go backstage when she finished her set."

"Let's say the pretty songbird looks out for our interests."

"I see. I appreciate you coming."

Scott paused before walking out the door. "Tell me one thing—what were they searching for?"

"I can only tell you that they didn't find it."

"Was it bigger than a bread basket?"

"Good day to you, sir," Mona said coldly.

Scott put on his hat and tipped the brim. "Until we meet again, Miss Mona." He nodded to Violet. "Miss Violet."

As soon as he closed the door, Violet ran and locked it.

"I don't think locks will keep these people out."

"It will sure slow them down."

Mona laughed. "I think a furniture barricade each night might be the answer."

"Miss Mona, please let us go home."

"I explained why we can't. I don't want to bring this trouble back to Kentucky."

"Can you tell me what they were looking for?" Violet said, picking up pieces from a broken lamp.

"They were looking for a file."

"What file?"

"Believe me, if I could tell you, Violet, I would. Now go get Jamison and Samuel. I will explain what I can, but you are just going to have to trust me."

Violet hesitated for a moment and then decided that Mona must have her reasons. She did as bidden and went for Jamison and Samuel.

Mona took the free moment to go out on the balcony and breathe in the fresh air. She noticed a man hanging about a street lamp across the boulevard, smoking a cigarette. Mona knew instantly that he was watching her suite. No doubt there were several men watching the hotel, but were they the good guys or the bad guys? And were the good guys really good?

All Mona knew for sure was that everyone was upping the ante and starting to play rough.

Well, she could play rough, too.

15

Rupert Hunt knocked on the door of Miss Nasha Martin.

Miss Martin answered the door in a powder blue dressing gown hanging off her left shoulder. Her hair was not combed and lipstick was smeared across her face. Leaning lazily against the door jam, she yawned and asked, "What do you want, pal?"

"My employer would like to speak with you."

"Not interested," Martin said as she tried to slam the door shut, but Hunt put his foot in the door.

"I'll scream," Martin hissed, her eyes opening wide with fear.

"Would this help ease your anxiety?" Hunt asked, holding up a crisp fifty-dollar bill.

"Is it for real?" Martin asked, grabbing at the bill.

Hunt pulled the money out of her reach. "Sure is."

"Not counterfeit?"

"Genuine money. Now will you see my employer?"

"Sure," Miss Martin said, seizing the bill and sticking it down her gown between her cleavage. "Whatcha want?"

Hunt stepped back, allowing Mona Moon to enter the apartment. He then stepped inside and closed the door.

Mona quickly took in a neat apartment which was in contrast to Miss Martin's disheveled appearance. The sofa and chair were newly upholstered in cheerful chintz and an expensive Philco radio console sat in the corner. There were several worn books on the end tables, even Emily Post's book on etiquette. Martin was a woman who was hell bent on improving herself. Besides a few empty gin bottles and two dirty glasses, everything looked neat, tidy, and in good condition. Rare for apartments now-a-days when most abodes were peeling paint from maintenance neglect due to the Depression.

Miss Martin put her hands on her hips and declared, "Didn't expect someone like you."

"May I sit?" Mona asked.

"Please yourself, honey." Martin lit a cigarette and looked around for a glass with stale gin. Blowing smoke into the air, she said, "Sorry, I don't have anything to offer besides water and milk. Looks like all the gin is gone. Had a small party last night."

"That's quite all right. I shan't be here long."

Martin gave Mona's smart gray tailored suit and a hat sporting a veil a quick once-over. "Listen, let's cut to the quick. Okay, honey? I didn't know your man was married."

Lifting her veil over the hat, Mona smiled. "I'm not here about that, but I do have some questions for you."

"Fifty dollars got you in the door. Want information? That will cost you more." Martin folded her arms and gave Mona a defiant look.

Mona glanced over at Hunt and nodded.

He stepped forward with another crisp fifty-dollar bill, which Martin snatched from him.

Feeling slightly embarrassed at her greed, Martin explained, "Times are hard for black gals. Gotta do what you can."

"Times are hard for women everywhere—not just black women. Listen, I'm not here to talk politics per se. I need to know if you know a man by the name of Abraham Scott."

Miss Martin pulled her dressing wrap tighter and sat down in a chair across from Mona. "Maybe. What's it to you?"

"I need to know if he is capable of murder."

"He's got you in a jam, has he? Who are you exactly?"

"You don't need to know my name. I just want information, and then I'll be out of your way."

"I know who you are. You can't fool me with that black wig and veil. It's them yellow eyes that betray you. I've seen your picture in the papers. Read that you have golden eyes. You're Mona Moon. You're rich. You can do better than a lousy hundred. I've got rent coming up."

"If you think that I am Mona Moon, then you know that I am a woman who can help you. What do you desire?"

"You can't do nothing for me, lady, besides

give me more money. I suggest you leave if you know what's good for you."

Undeterred, Mona continued, "I know your real name is Lillyrose Strum from North Carolina."

Martin looked surprised. "I thought Nasha Martin sounded more refined."

"You have a mother sick with consumption and a brother in prison for stealing food from a local grocery store. Now what is your great desire?"

Martin took in Mona from her tailored day suit to her silk stocking that showed no sign of mending. "I want to retire by the age of forty, have a place in Harlem for my mother and me, and have my own car."

"I can arrange for you to record your own music like Bessie Smith does. Since you know who I am, you know I can deliver."

"How can I trust you to keep your word?"

"You can't, but you have nothing to lose if you do so."

"Perhaps my life."

"You're playing a game now. Let's not be so dramatic."

Martin thought for a moment. "You're right. I have nothing to lose."

"Who is Abraham Scott to you?"

"He is my handler. I pick up men from various embassies at the club. They all come to see me. They think I'm exotic, especially those from Europe. I listen to their drunken ramblings and report to Scott, but he's cheap. Only pays me five dollars per tip. I can't get to Harlem on that."

"And what have you told him?"

"Everyone is talking about Gloria Vanderbilt."

"What else?" Mona asked, not interested in Little Gloria's custody case between her mother, Gloria Morgan Vanderbilt and aunt, Gertrude Vanderbilt Whitney.

"The Americans talk about the dust storms in the Midwest and the bad economy. The French talk about French-Indochina, and the British talk about the Prince of Wales."

"What do the Germans talk about?"

"They talk about power and how to use it. They make bold predictions."

"What kind of predictions?"

"Some nonsense about the Third Reich lasting

for a thousand years. I don't even know what that is. They are always boasting."

"Did the subject of copper ever come up?"

Martin thought for a moment. "You know there have been so many men and so many conversations to remember."

Irritated, Mona nodded to Hunt, who produced another fifty-dollar bill.

"No more hustling, Miss Martin, or that record producer won't get a call."

Seeing she couldn't push Mona further, Martin said, "All right. I'll drop a dime, but you can't breathe a word to Scott that I talked to you. You gotta promise me."

"He'll never know."

"Well, then," Martin said cautiously, "I was a hostess at a card game with some Germans, and they were talking about needing certain minerals for mass manufacturing. They didn't know I have a German boyfriend, and that I knew a little German, so I played dumb."

"What did the men say?"

"They were having trouble getting access to copper and tin. Companies were hesitant to sell to them, but they had struck a deal with Sweden."

"Was my name or Moon Enterprises mentioned?"

"No, but they said they were going to put pressure on American owners to sell them copper."

"You said you have a German boyfriend. Is this boyfriend, Otto Mueller?"

Martin looked surprised. "Yeah, but I haven't seen him for a while. I'm getting kind of worried."

Mona resisted an urge to glance at Hunt. Martin didn't know that Otto Mueller was dead. Mona forged ahead. "What does Mr. Mueller tell you?"

"Not much. He always wants to talk about the music. He is a real lover of jazz. Says I have talent." Martin took a sip of old gin from one of the dirty glasses. "Only person to really believe in me." Martin's voice turned soft when speaking of Mueller.

"He tells you nothing of Germany's plans for the future?"

"Doesn't like to talk about it except that he feels the country is going in the wrong direction. Otto was forced to join the Nazi party. He needs his job as he had a family to support."

"You know he is married?"

"He told me, but I don't hold that against him. Says his wife is a wonderful woman, but they just don't have common interests. His relationship with me has nothing to do with her." Looking wistful, Martin added, "His family still lives in Germany. Otto will only be here for another year before he retires and goes back home."

"Is he ever joined by a man named Lars Dardel—a Swede—young, blond hair with handsome features?"

"Yeah. On occasion."

"What's his connection to Otto Mueller?"

"They both come to the club to hear me sing. Dardel also loves music, though I think he is more of a classical music fan. I think he comes to please Otto."

"What is Mr. Mueller's job and where does he work?"

"At the German Embassy. He transcribes foreign letters and cables—summarizing the information for upper management. Otto speaks Swedish, English, and Italian."

"So he has access to high level information."

Martin laughed, "Oh heavens no. Nothing of real importance. He doesn't have the security clearance."

"Does he talk about copper or ever mention me by name?" Mona asked again.

"Not that I recall. Otto doesn't like to talk shop when he is with me. He likes to discuss music and my list of songs for the night. That type of thing. The conversation is usually about me."

"Does he carry an attaché case with him? Bring it here?"

Martin shook her head. "I never saw a case."

"Does he meet Lars Dardel away from the club or your apartment?"

"I don't know. Ask Otto." Miss Martin looked disgruntled. "I'll tell you one thing about Lars Dardel. He can't keep his hands off the ladies. Know what I mean?"

"Explain it to me."

"The waitresses at the club hate him. He's always grabbing them or trying to play kissy face. He even tried to lure me away from Otto."

"Did you tell Scott about Dardel's behavior?"

"Yeah, but he didn't seem too interested."

"What about Otto? Did you tell him?"

"Why are you asking all these questions about Otto? I thought you wanted to know about Abraham Scott."

"Is Otto Mueller your friend's real name?"

"Hey, what goes on here?" Martin asked, looking back and forth between Mona and Hunt.

"Curious, that's all. One more thing."

"What?"

"Does Otto Mueller know that you work for Abraham Scott?"

"Are you crazy? Of course, he doesn't, and you're not gonna spill the beans and mess up a good thing!"

Mona rose. "Thank you for your time, Miss Martin. Mr. Hunt will be in touch when the record deal is set."

"You won't forget?"

"I'll keep my end of the bargain. You keep yours. Not a word to anyone that I was here."

Martin nodded.

Mona motioned to Hunt to leave with her.

As soon as they had exited the building from the back entrance, Hunt stopped Mona. "Why didn't you tell Martin about Otto's death? She doesn't even know that Dardel is dead as well."

"That's Scott's job. If he hasn't told her already, it's because he's waiting for something. Perhaps he doesn't want to frighten her. It's not my job to bust his chops."

"She's lying, you know."

"On some things, yes, but not all. I think she was rather fond of Otto Mueller even though she was spying on him for Abraham Scott. One thing is for sure, Otto Mueller was not some low-level bureaucrat. He was high up in the German command."

"It's for sure that Otto Mueller was not this man's real name. If he was a member of the Nazi party and caught with a black woman . . ." Hunt drew a line across his throat with his index finger. "Goodbye, Herr Mueller."

"The British got to him first. I kind of feel sorry for the man. He was caught in a trap."

"I think the girl was just a cover. I think old Otto was there to meet up with people and pass on information."

"You think Mueller was a spy? Spying for whom?"

Hunt shrugged. "Maybe the Russians. Perhaps if you gave me all the facts, I can come up with a reasonable hypothesis."

"I'm not at liberty to discuss everything with you, but I'll give you an A for effort for trying to catch me off guard."

Hunt grinned. "Just thought I might glean a little tidbit."

"Let's just stick with the facts as you know them. There has been no mention of Russians in any of this mess."

"Okay, just thinking out loud." Hunt switched to another topic. "Are you serious about this record deal?"

"I will keep my word unless Martin double crosses me."

"What do you want me to do?"

"Have Miss Martin followed. I want to know whom she sees and where she goes."

"That means more men."

"So hire them."

"You're the boss lady, but it's going to cost a pretty penny."

"Don't worry, Rupert. I've got the penny, copper at that, and more to spare," Mona said, pulling down her veil.

Rupert Hunt laughed as they walked down an alleyway. Once they came to the main thoroughfare, he went one way and Mona the other.

16

"What are you looking at?" Violet asked.

Mona was sitting at a table marking off names from a list. "Rupert got the passenger manifests from all the outgoing ocean liners from five to three days ago. I'm looking for German sounding names."

"And then what?"

Mona pointed to a stack of Portsmouth and London newspapers. "Go through those and look for any articles about a passenger dying or falling overboard on one of these passenger ships."

"Looking for anyone specifically?"

"There can't be too many deaths on a ship. Pull them all out."

"Are you sure about Portsmouth papers? Why there?"

"Because most intercontinental sea voyages begin in New York and end in Portsmouth, Great Britain."

Violet said, "German ships sometimes dock in Portugal or Spain."

"If you can't find anything in these papers, we will widen our search."

"Are you sure you have the right time frame? Any kind of news about a death would only be reported after the ship landed."

"I think this death will be reported earlier."

"Why?"

"Just have my suspicions, that's all." Mona couldn't tell Violet that the body, smuggled out of the Willard Hotel in a steamer trunk, was placed aboard an ocean liner, and unceremoniously dumped in the middle of the Atlantic Ocean.

"I don't see what ocean liner passenger lists have to do with anything."

Mona didn't repeat what Abraham Scott confided in her about what his men did with Otto Mueller's corpse. The less Violet knew, the better.

"If I were you, I'd look in the Washington obituaries," Violet suggested.

Mona looked up from her list with a pencil poised in her hand. "Will you do that as well, Violet?"

"Sure."

Violet spent the next twenty-five minutes going through New York, Baltimore, and Washington newspapers until she came to a small article only two paragraphs long. "Miss Mona, I think I found something in the New York Herald Tribune."

Mona pushed back in her chair. "Great. Read it out loud, please."

Mr. Alburn Bower, 54, died on the SS Cathay, presumably by drowning. Witnesses say Mr. Bower slipped, lost his balance, and fell overboard. His body was not recovered. Mr. Bower is survived by his wife, Anna Schafer Bower, 51, and three children, Thomas, 21, Jorg, 15, and Jakob, 10. Mr. Bower worked for the German Embassy in Washington, D.C. as an interpreter. His colleagues express their condolences to his family and friends at his passing.

"Is that what you were looking for?"
"Yes, it is."

"May I be excused then? Hilda and I are going to the Smithsonian Museum this afternoon."

"Take one of the Pinkertons with you."

Violet sighed. "Do I have to? I don't want some man following us. Hilda will spot him and that will blow my cover with her."

Mona chuckled. "You have a cover now, do you?"

Violet grinned. "You know what I mean."

"Sorry, but no one can leave the hotel without someone accompanying them. It's for your own protection, especially you. Tell him not to follow too closely. Hilda won't even notice. Besides, with all the kidnapping going on in the world, she probably expects the companion of a rich woman to have some sort of bodyguard."

"Okay. I'll inform the Pinkertons that I'm going out. What about you?"

"I'm going to bed with a good mystery. A new Dorothy L. Sayers mystery just came out titled *The Nine Tailors*. I can't wait to read it."

Violet hesitated a second before stating, "Hilda and I might go to a movie after the museum."

"That's fine, Violet. You deserve a break. I shan't need you tonight."

"Thank you. I won't be too late."

"Don't forget your new hat and gloves," Mona said as she went back to her list.

"I think I might take an umbrella too. It looks like rain."

"Un huh," Mona mumbled, distracted.

Seeing that Mona was not paying attention, Violet saw her chance to escape.

"Have fun," Mona murmured as Violet grabbed her things, slipped out the door, and scooted past the Pinkertons to downstairs where Hilda waited.

Giggling, Violet sneaked out through the employee's entrance with Hilda without thinking anyone would notice her leaving the hotel.

Violet thought wrong.

As soon as Violet and Hilda left the hotel, they were followed by two hired thugs with orders to harm the girls.

17

The butler opened the door of the British Embassy.

"I would like to see Ambassador Lindsay, please." A furious Mona handed the butler her card. "Tell him Miss Mona Moon is here."

The butler looked at the card and handed it back to Mona. "I'm afraid His Lordship is not at home, miss."

"Then I'll wait." Mona pushed past the small-statured butler, as did Jamison and Samuel.

Flabbergasted, the butler sputtered, "This, this is most unseemly, miss. I will have to call the staff and have you forcibly removed."

"You can try, sir, but this man right here . . ." Mona said, pointing to Samuel.

The butler gazed at Samuel's tall stature and imposing physique.

Teasing, Samuel leaned in and gave the butler the evil eye.

Alarmed, the butler drew back.

Samuel tried not to laugh at the butler's confused expression. He guessed many people didn't try to break into the British Embassy. Only his boss would have the moxie to do so.

Mona said, "He is a noted boxing champion where I come from. He'll give your lads a bloody nose for sure."

"And I'll help him," Jamison chimed in.

"JOHN! What the devil is going on? What's all this racket?"

Mona looked up to see Sir Lindsay, wearing a smoking jacket, peering over the second floor banister. Her angry gaze returned to the butler, she said, "So the Ambassador is not home, huh?"

"Miss Moon and her henchmen are threatening to throttle me, sir," the butler whined.

Lindsay chuckled. "No one is going to lay a hand on you, John."

"I tried my best, sir, to shoo them away, but they won't leave. Miss Moon insists upon seeing you."

"I want to see you, Ambassador! Right now!"

Mona yelled at Lindsay.

Lindsay showed surprise. People usually did not shout at him and make demands, especially at this time of night, but then this was America where there was a lack of respect for authority. "It's late, Miss Moon. Can you come back tomorrow?"

Mona noticed some of the household staff had meandered into the foyer. Several of them were wearing their nightclothes. "Shall I accuse you of a dastardly act in front of everyone or would you like to hear me out in private?"

"I have no idea what you are sputtering!"

"Sure you do." Mona glared up at Lindsay.

"Very well, then. John, show Miss Moon to my library. I'll be down in a moment."

"Shall I have tea made, sir?"

"How about a sedative for Miss Moon?" Lindsay said, before heading off to change.

Fearful at how Mona would react, the butler immediately tried to distract her. "This way, miss."

Mona did not move.

The butler begged, "Please, miss. It's been a very long day."

Realizing she was putting the butler through some discomfort, she acquiesced. "Show me the way, John."

The butler's face brightened. "Follow me, miss."

Mona turned to Samuel and Jamison. "You two can cool your heels right here."

Happy to do so, they both nodded.

Mona followed John to the library and poured herself a bourbon.

"Would you like tea, miss?"

"No, thank you. I shan't be long."

"Thank God," the butler muttered on his way out.

Overhearing him, Mona chuckled. She knew she was a hellion when angry. Mona sank into an overstuffed chair and took a big swig of her drink. Her nerves were raw, but this matter couldn't wait.

Moments later, Lindsay entered the library wearing a dark gray suit with a blue and gold tie. Seeing that Mona was imbibing bourbon, Lindsay poured himself a sherry. "Cheers," he said, before taking a drink. Noting that Mona's face was still flush, he was curious as to her intention. "Miss

Moon, to what do I owe this honor?"

Mona put her drink down. "I've had enough, Sir Lindsay."

"Enough of what?"

"You're to leave my people alone."

Lindsay set his glass down. "I'm sorry, but I don't know what you mean."

"I just collected my companion, Miss Violet Tate, and her friend from the police station. They had been brutally attacked by some thugs who ripped their frocks, stockings, and said lewd things to them. These girls were punched in the face, Sir Lindsay. PUNCHED! If you want to get into a pissing contest with me, fine, but don't take your anger and frustration out on two innocent girls or any of my employees. You deal with me directly."

Lindsay said, "I have no idea what you are talking about, Miss Moon. I am truly sorry for this unfortunate incident, but why lay this at my door?"

"Because Miss Tate and the other girl said the men spoke with British accents."

Lindsay's eyes widened.

"I bet that if they could see a lineup of your

male staff, they could identify these miscreants."

"Miss Moon, I know that you are upset, but I will not be accused of orchestrating an assault on vulnerable young women. How dare you!"

"I'm not finished. My suite at the Willard was ransacked several days ago. A little bird told me that it was your men who did the dirty deed. Apparently they were looking for something."

Lindsay shot up from his chair. "I will not stand for this!"

Mona stood up as well. "You stay away from my people and me, or I'll go to the papers with this."

"They wouldn't print a word of it. It's too fantastic."

"No? All I have to do is have Lord Farley make a few disparaging remarks to the British press about your competency and see what happens then. Once the papers get a whiff of something, they are like bloodhounds. They'll keep digging until they come up with something." She handed Lindsay her empty glass. "And don't even think to plant drugs or a hot gun on me and then tip off the police. I am wise to those tricks."

Mona moved to the library door. "I'll see myself out." She quietly closed the door and left the embassy with Jamison and Samuel shadowing her.

Lindsay sat down and finished his sherry. All he could utter was, "My word, how extraordinary!"

18

"How bad is it?" Violet asked, tearfully, the next morning.

Mona scrutinized Violet's face. "It's not too bad. A little makeup should cover those bruises. Violet, I want you to know I lodged a complaint with Sir Lindsay."

"When?"

"Last night after you went to bed. Samuel, Jamison, and I paid the Ambassador a visit. If the men who attacked you were British, Lindsay will investigate it. We'll find out who did this."

"I was so frightened. Those men came out of nowhere."

"It wouldn't have happened if you had followed my instructions, Violet. You sneaked out without informing the Pinkertons. Those hoodlums were following you, and when they saw you didn't have a guard detail with you, decided to close in."

"Samuel left the Willard without a detail," Violet said, sullenly.

"He doesn't do that anymore. I think everyone realizes that the men who want our copper play for keeps."

"If only you would tell us everything. I know you're holding back."

"You are on a need-to-know basis. I am not at liberty to discuss certain things with you. If you insist on staying a nosey little girl, then I'm sending you home—today!"

Violet's eyes widened. "Please don't do that, Miss Mona. If my mother sees my face bruised up like this, she will never let me leave Moon Manor again. I'll be stuck on that farm until I'm thirty."

Mona wanted to chuckle, but didn't. This was a grave matter. Violet and Hilda could have been seriously injured or worse. She shuddered to think what those men might have done if bystanders hadn't heard the girls screaming and come to their aid.

A knock sounded on the door and Hilda poked her face in. "I'm going now, Miss Moon. Thank you for letting me stay the night in your suite. My folks would make me quit if they knew about last night. I told them I was working an extra shift and staying the night in the servant's quarters."

Noticing that Hilda had her maid uniform on, Mona said, "I don't think you are ready to go back to work yet."

Hilda nervously put her hands in her pockets. "I'm jeopardizing my position here. If Mrs. Ruttle knows that I went out with a guest and then spent the night in a suite, she would give me the heave-ho. I need this job, Miss Moon. I need to help my family. My father lost his job over a year ago, and he's now helping my mother take in laundry."

"I understand, Hilda, but I have planned a much better day for you and Violet. You both need to shake the cobwebs off."

"You're not going to send me away?" Violet asked, crossing her fingers.

"At least, not before I replace your dress."

"Oh." Violet understood that she was still on

thin ice with Mona.

"You two are to shop for new dresses with new hats, gloves, and stockings to match. In fact, get several pairs of stockings. Here is a list of things I need as well."

Mona noticed Hilda's fallen face.

"I can't afford a new dress, let alone a new hat and gloves."

"This is on me, Hilda. After last night, it's the least I can do."

"How will I explain a new outfit to my folks?"

Mona handed Hilda her card. "Give this to your parents and tell them to call me if they have any questions."

"I don't want them to know about last night. They'd blame me."

"Tell them it is a treat from me, an eccentric rich woman from Kentucky, for your help during my stay in Washington. If they call, that's what I'll tell them."

"But my job? I'm supposed to report in ten minutes."

"I'll call Mrs. Ruttle and ask her if it is all right for you to help Violet run errands for me. She'll be fine with it."

Violet and Hilda shot gleeful peeks at each other before they returned their attention to Mona. "Now if any of the Pinkertons tell me that either one of you disobeys his orders, then I'll take back the outfits. Do we have a deal?"

"Yes, ma'am," they chorused.

"Good. I've already set up an appointment at a store in town. One of their clerks will assist you and send me the bill. Jamison will drive you."

Mona turned and picked up the morning paper, thinking the dressing down was over. She wanted to eat the breakfast Samuel had prepared for her in peace.

When Violet and Hilda still stood looking expectantly at her, Mona said, "You are both excused. Hilda, borrow a dress from Violet."

"Yes, miss," Hilda answered, before excitedly running after Violet, who was already making a beeline for her room.

Mona watched the girls eagerly rush off and couldn't help but smile. She remembered when Dexter Deatherage had her stop off in Cincinnati for a shopping spree before heading to Lexington after she had inherited the Moon millions. It was the first time Mona had unlimited money to shop for nice clothes. Before she had haunted bazaars and thrift shops for the outfits on her back. She recalled how excited she had been to pick out evening gowns with matching shoes and day dresses made of material that was soft to her skin. A new frock to a woman was like strolling in heaven.

At least, that's what Mona thought.

19

Rupert Hunt was giving Mona a rundown of the daily adventures of Nasha Martin when Samuel announced the arrival of Alice Longworth and Lady Lindsay. "I had them wait in the foyer."

"I wonder what they want," Mona said.

"I'll just hide in Violet's room. By the way, where is she?"

"She went to the drugstore to purchase some makeup to go with her new outfit. She went on a shopping spree this morning. Now she wants to cover the marks on her face." Mona saw Rupert's anxious expression. "Don't worry. She has a Pinkerton with her."

Rupert looked relieved. "Good. I'll keep the door propped open a bit, so I can eavesdrop."

"Always the snoop."

Rupert grinned before heading to the bedroom. "That's my job."

Noting that Rupert was now out of sight, Mona nodded to Samuel to bring them into the sitting room.

Alice burst into the room with such energy that papers flew off the table. "So sorry to arrive unannounced, but Lady Lindsay has something to say to you." She turned to Lady Lindsay, who crept into the room slowly and sheepishly looked about. "Don't you, Elizabeth?"

Lady Lindsay nodded. "May we sit?"

Mona said, "Of course. Please."

Alice and Lady Lindsay sat on a settee together.

Mona, Alice, and Lady Lindsay sat quietly, glancing at one another until Mona spoke, "To what do I owe this honor?"

Alice elbowed Lady Lindsay. "Get on with it."

Lady Lindsay cleared her throat. "I understand that you visited my husband several nights ago and accused him of having your suite ransacked and your companion attacked."

"Her maid," Alice insisted.

Mona shot Alice a harsh look. "Are you here to intercede for Ambassador Lindsay? I am thinking of making a formal complaint against him with the British government and nothing you say will change my mind. You should see my companion's face and the face of the girl who was with her. Barbaric, I tell you."

Lady Lindsay lowered her head and reached into her purse for a handkerchief. Dabbing her eyes, she said, "Ronald is a good man. A worthy man. He does not deserve your condemnation. I was the one who gave the order for your suite to be ransacked, but I did not order the destruction of your property."

"Those men took all our silk stockings, my garter belt, and other female apparel, not to mention sedating my bodyguard team. Most unseemly, Lady Lindsay. Not the cowboy way."

"I will replace all items they took. I'm so sorry. They just got carried away."

"Who were they?"

"Two gentlemen who work for the British government. That's all I will say on the matter."

"And you swear on the Bible that Ambassador Lindsay had no knowledge of this action?"

"I swear he did not."

"Does he now?"

Lady Lindsay shook her head.

"What were you searching for?"

"You know what. I never should have given you that report on Dardel. The very next day, Lindsay's secretary was turning the embassy upside down searching for it. I must have it back."

"Why didn't you just ask me for it?"

Lady Lindsay's eyes widened. "You would have given it back?"

"Sure. I already had a photostat made of it."

"Oh dear," Lady Lindsay said, her brow gathering.

Alice nudged Lady Lindsay again. "Elizabeth, make peace, not war."

"May I have the original file?"

"First you need to tell me why you had my companion and her friend attacked?"

Lady Lindsay cast a shocked looked at Alice, who looked dumbfounded as well. "I'm afraid I don't know what you are talking about. I never had your staff attacked."

Alice butted in. "This is the first we've heard

of this. Someone attacked Bucktooth Becky? How is she?"

"Bruised up a bit. They punched her in the face."

"What did they say? What did they want?"

Mona replied, "She doesn't really know. It happened so fast, and she couldn't understand what they were saying because their English accents were so thick."

Alice asked, "Violet said they had English accents?"

Lady Lindsay shook her head. "This can not be laid at my doorstep, nor Ronald's. He would never order an attack on any woman."

Frustrated, Alice asked again, "What type of accents? Upper class English accents, Cockney, Irish, Welch, Scottish, Yorkshire."

"She doesn't know, Alice."

"Perhaps it was a mugging," Lady Lindsay suggested.

Mona replied, "I don't think so. They didn't grab their purses. They just roughed them up. I hate to think of what would have happened if some passersby hadn't heard those girls scream for help."

"I know everything that goes on at the embassy. It wasn't one of our people," Lady Lindsay said.

Mona didn't reply as she really didn't believe Lady Lindsay. "Are we finished?"

"I must have that report back. I can not have my husband know that I gave you a confidential report, Miss Mona. It would seriously jeopardize my marriage and his trust in me."

"Come on, Mona. You got what you needed from that report. Give it back," Alice coerced.

Mona sighed. "Very well. Follow me." Mona took them to the end of the hallway and into the small kitchen that accompanied the suites on that floor. Next to the window were several crates of Coca-Cola. Mona pulled up all the bottles from the first crate and reached in for the file. She handed it to Lady Lindsay.

Alice whistled and said, "Clever girl. How did you know that no one would look there?"

"I didn't. I just figured that anyone looking for the file wouldn't bother looking through all the crates. When they came looking, this crate was on the bottom of three crates. My butler loves his soda pop. As you can see, he has gone through an entire crate on his own and now this crate is on top."

Lady Lindsay put the file in a leather portfolio she brought with her. "Thank you, Mona. I hope we can put this unpleasantness behind us and move forward."

When Mona didn't respond, Alice took the hint. "I see that there is some more damage control to be done here, but let's leave on a positive note. Come, Elizabeth. We've taken up enough of Mona's time."

"Yes, of course."

Alice said, "Go on, dear, I'll be along in a moment."

Samuel appeared out of nowhere. "Lady Lindsay, may I escort you to the elevator?"

"Yes, thank you." She turned to Mona and mouthed, *thank you again*, before following Samuel out of the kitchen.

Alice waited until Lady Lindsay was out of earshot before she turned to Mona. "Lars Dardel's funeral will be tomorrow. Bring Violet along and see if she recognizes anyone. I want the fiend who pummeled my Bucktooth Becky punished."

"Violet would be touched about your concern of her welfare."

Alice scoffed. "We can't have hooligans roughing up the lower classes. How ever shall we keep maids if this continues?"

Mona flashed a wide smile. "Alice, you are a burnt marshmallow—crusty on the outside and gooey on the inside. You are fooling no one. I'll tell Violet that you are worried about her."

"I am not! It's just that good help is hard to find." Alice swung the tail of her fox stole around her neck and stormed off with Mona's laughter ringing in her ears.

20

Mona and Violet silently crept into the church moments before the funeral began. Sitting in a side aisle of the large cathedral, they were able to see the faces of most of those attending. Mona recognized Ambassador Boström from his pictures in the newspaper. He took a seat close to the front with other official looking people after saying a few words to Mrs. Dardel who was standing near her husband's coffin.

"Should we pay our respects to the widow?" Violet asked.

"I might speak to her after the funeral, but I want to see who talks to her."

"Let's sit closer. You might recognize the two assailants if you heard their voices again."

"Part of me would rather not, but another

part of me wants to see them go to jail."

"That's the spirit, Violet." Mona clasped Violet's hands and gave a quick squeeze before returning her attention to the crowd.

Violet smiled at Mona. Nothing seemed to keep Mona Moon down. Not even the fact that Lord Farley had arrived safely in Great Britain and had not seen fit to call or even send a telegram. Mona never asked if he had called or even mentioned his name. Violet wished she could be more like her.

They inched their way closer to the main huddle of mourners. They sat on the very left of the nave. Mona casually took out her powder compact and fussed with her hair looking in the mirror, in order to see who was sitting behind her.

She closed it when the redheaded ingénue from the British Embassy party sashayed into the cathedral. She caused quite a sensation with her brightly colored yellow coat covering a blue serge dress and an orchid wrist corsage. The woman looked like she was going to a party and not a funeral. Noting she was causing quite a stir, the actress took her place among the mourners.

Mona and Violet quickly looked to see how Mrs. Dardel reacted to the captivating starlet. Disappointingly, the widow was conversing with the priest, who was about to deliver the eulogy.

"Who is that dreadful woman?" Violet asked.

"She's a British subject on way her to Hollywood. She was at the embassy's party. Dardel danced with her."

"What's her name?"

Mona thought for a moment. "To tell you the truth, I can't remember. I'm surprised she is here. Dardel overreached himself when he danced with her. He put his hand on her derriere. She seemed to be very angry about it at the time."

"Maybe that's why she's smiling now. She wants to make sure he's dead."

"Hush, you two, and move over."

Mona and Violet looked up to see Alice Roosevelt Longworth hovering impatiently over them. They moved over to allow her a seat in the pew.

"Why are you sitting all the way over here? This is not where the action is."

"So we can observe without being observed ourselves."

Alice grabbed Violet's face and twisted it toward her. "Let me see what those monsters did, Bucktooth Becky."

Violet tried to pull away but couldn't.

"Oh, goodness, they really did a number on you," Alice complained.

"Looks better than it did. I've got makeup on."

"You need to apply it more thickly. Didn't do much for you. The purple shows through."

Mona wanted to groan at Alice's intrusion but it was too late. People were already turning in their seats trying to gauge who was causing all the racket. As soon as they saw Alice, they waved and turned back in their seats. No way were they going to scold her. Not Alice Roosevelt Longworth. They'd rather set their tongues on fire.

Mrs. Dardel sat in the front pew with an older woman who Mona assumed was Dardel's mother. The priest began the service. Wanting to get a better view of who was at the service, Mona maneuvered across Violet and Alice into the side aisle and hid behind a massive column. Upon hearing soft footsteps behind, she was too late in turning.

As a hand clapped tightly across her mouth, Mona heard, "It's just me. Didn't want to startle you coming up behind."

Mona clamped down on a tiny bit of flesh on the palm with her teeth.

"Wow whee," the man hissed as he jerked his hand away.

Mona pulled out her powder compact and checked her lipstick. It was smeared. "You've mussed my face." She took out a handkerchief to fix her lips and then put on a fresh coat of lipstick. "Want do you want?"

Scott bowed. "My apologies, good lady. It was not my intention. We need to talk."

Mona took off her shoes before heading to the foyer of the cathedral. She made sure she softly closed the main door behind her.

Scott followed.

Once outside, Mona leaned on Scott to put her shoes back on.

"That was thoughtful of you."

"I certainly didn't want the mourners to hear the clicking of my heels on the marble floor during the service."

"As if there are any mourners in there," Scott

said, thumbing at the sanctuary.

"His wife seems torn up."

"Perhaps the only one."

"I'm surprised that Dardel was a Catholic and not a Lutheran."

"His wife is Catholic. I've always thought that's why Dardel took such chances. His wife's religion didn't go down well with Dardel's bosses, and he tried to increase his prospects of a promotion by taking risky assignments. The problem was he was so terrible at being a spy." Scott gave a short chortle.

"Then I'm surprised the priest agreed to perform the funeral if Dardel was not officially Catholic."

"His wife is a big donor to this particular parish," Scott said, winking.

"Still, Dardel must have been well-liked for so many people to come to his funeral."

"If he had been well-liked, the church would have been filled. Most of the women here were discarded dalliances of his. And the others? Well, let's say they work for me."

"Ambassador Boström is attending."

"Only because it would look bad if he didn't.

Hey, Mona, don't waste your time feeling sorry for this guy. He's not worth your pity."

"It's just that he was so pathetic, but I do feel sorry for his wife. I was at Ambassador Lindsay's party when Dardel made a move on a Hollywood hopeful. She's inside the church now."

"She is Lisa LaMour."

"Oh dear."

"That's what I say. Not very subtle, is it? Her real name is Zofia Kowalsky. Her family immigrated to England after the last war."

Organ music from the church floated outside and the front doors were swept open by the altar boys.

"That was a quick funeral." Mona turned to Scott. "Did you find out who attacked Violet Tate?"

"Have dinner with me tonight, and I'll tell you."

Curious, Mona said, "All right, but I'll meet you."

"Okay. Come to the jazz club around nine."

"The only thing they serve there is gin."

"They fry up a mean ribeye and skillet potatoes."

"Sure they do," Mona said sarcastically, wondering what Scott was up to.

"You'll see."

"I need to go inside. I want to speak with Mrs. Dardel."

"See you tonight." Scott tipped his hat before walking away.

Mona called after him. "Hey, Scott."

"Yeah," he said turning.

"I usually go for my gun when men touch me without permission."

Grinning, Scott said, "Noted."

Mona nodded and went back into the church, darting between the clumps of people chitchatting in the aisles. She found Violet sitting in the same pew waiting for her. Alice was up front and center chatting with Ambassador Boström. The poor widow sat grief stricken looking on as the priest closed the casket. Mona felt pity for her and the woman sitting next to her.

She went up to the widow. "Mrs. Dardel. My name is Mona Moon. I would like to express my condolences." Mona turned to the older woman, who looked as though she was in a state of shock. Her eyes had the appearance of someone suddenly surprised as she stared at the coffin. "I assume that you are Mr. Dardel's mother. Very sorry for your loss, ma'am."

Mrs. Dardel looked up through tear stained eyes. "My mother-in-law doesn't speak English."

"Oh, I see."

"Who are you?"

"I met your husband at Ambassador Lindsay's party. We talked briefly about Sweden purchasing copper ore from my mines." Mona noticed Mrs. Dardel wore her watch on her right wrist and her black mourning band was on her right forearm.

"That's what your conversation was about?" Mrs. Dardel asked rather pointedly.

"Yes, it was about copper."

"I saw the two of you on the patio having quite the cozy yak."

"That's correct. We spoke on the patio."

Was Mrs. Dardel implying something? Mona wasn't sure of the undertone of Mrs. Dardel's statement. "Have the police caught the culprit yet?"

"No and they never will. Lars has officially died of heart issues. I had to agree to this false report, or the British threatened to say that Lars committed suicide. If they did that, Lars wouldn't be permitted to be buried in consecrated ground."

"Mr. Dardel is being buried in a Catholic cemetery?"

"That's how they control people. They find a weak spot and exploit it. The truth almost never comes out."

"Who are *they*, Mrs. Dardel?"

"They thought they knew everything, but they didn't," Mrs. Dardel said, looking at Mona triumphantly. "Lars was going to convert for me. Even this old bag sitting next to me didn't know. Her darling son. Huh! Lars hated her."

Mona was amazed at the confessions spewing from Mrs. Dardel's mouth. "Again, I'm so sorry."

"Go away, Miss Moon, and leave us to our grief. We don't know you and don't care to hear your lies."

Mona gave a small bow and retreated. She made her way to Violet, who was thumbing through a hymnal. "Let's go."

"Mrs. Longworth wants to go to lunch. Said she has something she wants to tell you. Says to meet up at the Old Ebbitt Grill in half an hour."

"Well, we do have to eat, and I don't like to partake any meals at our hotel unless Samuel fixes them."

Violet gave Mona a pleading look. "I'm starving."

"Let's go now. I could do with a cool drink."

"Can we order an appetizer? You know—just to take the edge off."

Mona teased, "I hear your stomach growling now. Let's hurry before you fall down due to lack of sustenance."

As they rushed out of the cathedral, Mona peeked back at Rupert Hunt, disguised as an old man surreptitiously taking pictures of everyone at the funeral. Even Violet didn't recognize him. Mona hoped he would have the photographs ready before nine that night.

Mona wanted all the ammunition she could get before her meeting with Scott.

At seven that night, Rupert Hunt reported to Mona. After listening to his report, Mona was loaded for bear.

21

Dressed in a gold lamé halter top dress that exposed her flawless back, Mona was shown to Scott's table. The dress was so tight-fitting, it would have shown evidence of undergarments had Mona been wearing any. The dress followed the curve of her waist and hips all the way down to her gold open-toed shoes. The top of the dress folded into several layers low on her chest, displaying alabaster skin. Mona's hair was pulled back into a bun twist fastened with golden-colored hairclips. Gold coiled serpentine bracelets encircled her upper arms. She wore no makeup except for the heavy kohl outlining her eyes and a lipstick tinted so deeply red, it almost looked black.

Scott jumped up as Mona was seated by the

waiter. "Wow, that is some dress! Lisa LaMour has nothing on you in the looks department."

"I never thought she did." Mona put her purse on the table with the clasp undone and facing her. "Buy me a drink, Scott."

"Abe, please."

"Like Honest Abe?"

"Maybe." Scott waved to a waiter who immediately rushed over.

"Yes, sir?"

"A bottle of your best champagne."

"Yes, sir!" The waiter hurried off to get the champagne. It was between the band's sets and he wanted to fill as many drink orders as possible because of the tips. Patrons were more likely to tip before the band played or they got too intoxicated to remember.

"I didn't think you were going to show."

Mona leaned forward. "I'm here as requested. What did you want to see me about?"

"This." Scott handed Mona a London newspaper.

"I've already seen the article."

"The one that stated that Lord Farley buried his father, and that the King and Queen of the

United Kingdom attended his father's funeral."

"Yes, I've read it."

"And?"

Mona shrugged. "And what? The man has buried his father according to the customs of his country. I don't know what you expect me to say."

"You weren't by his side."

"That's obvious."

Scott pointed to the picture in the paper. "That woman standing on the left of Lord Farley is Lady Alice, your best friend, and the chap standing next to her is her husband, Ogden Nithercott." Scott tapped on the picture. "Who's the lady on the right?"

Mona didn't even bother to look at the picture of the stylish young woman in a couture black dress hanging on to Robert's arm. Her head was covered in a long black veil. "You know who it is, so why ask?"

"Lord Farley is escorting this woman from the grave of his father."

"It's Lady Imogene. She is a distant cousin of Robert's."

"And she will inherit the estate if Lord Farley

does not produce an heir.”

“You are wrong there. If a male heir can’t be found, then the estate reverts back to the crown.”

The waiter brought the champagne and two glasses.

Scott waved him away.

Mona watched Scott uncork the champagne and pour it. She waited until he took a drink before she sipped from her glass.

“I see that you are being careful.”

“I don’t want to have happen to me what happened to my men.”

Scott held up his hands. “Innocent.”

“I believe you.” Mona took a short breath. “On that issue.”

“Let’s get back to Lady Imogene.”

“What about her?”

“It’s plain from the newspaper picture that she’s gunning for him. Even the article refers to their ‘close relationship.’”

Mona took another sip of her drink and didn’t reply.

“I thought you might be lonely.”

Mona laughed. “You couldn’t persuade me to be your spy by threats and intimidation. Now you are trying to seduce me? Oh, Scott."

"Call me Abe, Mona. Come on. Let's be friends. You know that English guy is not going to marry you. It's a different ball game for him now."

"I am interested in who attacked my little Violet."

"Still working on it. Don't have the answer for you yet."

"Well, I have been digging a little on my own." Mona pulled out some 3x5 snapshots from her purse. "Here's a picture of you having lunch with Lisa LaMour after the funeral."

Scott glanced at the picture. "Good shot of my profile. Sort of looks like John Barrymore."

Mona pulled out another one. "Here's another one of you meeting with a gentleman in the park two days ago. Looks like you are handing him something."

Scott picked up the photograph and tossed it back to her.

"This is my favorite. This was taken on the day after Dardel's murder. You were seen entering the Dardel household. To pay your respects to the grieving widow, no doubt?"

"That's right."

"I thought you were just aware of Dardel—you didn't give the impression that you knew him personally."

"Washington is a small town. Everyone knows everyone else."

"You never mentioned that you and he knew each other."

"Like I said, this is a small town."

"It's obvious that you knew him because here's a picture of you coming out the back entrance of the Swedish Embassy."

The last photograph made Scott uneasy, and he tried to change the subject.

"Why do you think the new Duke of Brynelleth has not even bothered to call or send you a cable?"

Not missing a beat, Mona pushed on. "I called William Donovan. You do not work for him. He says you are an independent agent who works for the highest bidder."

"I think Lawrence Robert Emerton Dagobert Farley has switched his loyalties."

"Who are you really? Is Abraham Scott even your real name?"

Seeing his ploy was not working, Scott admitted, "I never said I worked for William Donovan. I said I had been sent by President Roosevelt."

"Unofficially, like William Donovan? President Roosevelt doesn't even know that I exist, so why would he send you. Quit telling such lies. I'm sick of them."

"Believe me when I say President Roosevelt does know of your existence. My orders were to ferret out subversive affiliations or ideology that you might have. He and others are interested in how you turned Moon Enterprises around so fast in such a short amount of time. He wanted to know if you were the real deal or simply a naïve fool fronting for more sinister players."

"What others?"

"Men who are convinced there's going to be another world war. We are making a list of which Americans will step up to the plate when the time comes."

"Lots of things can happen before this so-called war of yours. Roosevelt could die. Hitler could die. I could die. No one can predict the future."

"We can predict probabilities. Here's a probability, Mona. Robert Farley has not communicated with you since his father died. From the looks of that newspaper photo, he has already replaced you with a woman, who's ten years younger and from one of the most ancient families in England. They are both British and descendants from the royal bloodline. Besides money, what do you have to offer the new Duke of Brynelleth? You can't overcome five hundred years of tradition."

Mona pushed the photographs she had taken of Scott toward him. "Keep the pictures, Abe. Put them in your scrapbook."

"Not going to crack, eh? Must be a blow to your ego, though. You're going to be thirty soon. Most people would call you a spinster. You're aging out of the marriage market."

"Whatever Robert Farley does is his own business, and I will support whatever he decides about his future."

Scott roared back in his chair. He was laughing so hard, he could barely get out the sentences, "Oh, you silly fool. You're already a laughing stock in town. Everyone thinks Robert Farley has already dumped you."

"That may be true, but my life doesn't revolve

around a man. If Lord Farley chooses to go down a different path, I wish him well, but I won't lose one night of sleep over it."

Scott stopped laughing. "You are a cold one, aren't you? You look cold, you know, with that white hair and strange eyes. Even your pale skin looks cool to the touch—flesh a corpse would have."

Mona gathered her purse. "You're a charmer, Abe. A real charmer." She stood, getting ready to take her leave. "Thanks for the champagne. See ya around."

Scott watched Mona walk away. He couldn't help admiring Mona's guts. She had a wild spirit no man could tame.

Walking out the door, Mona saw Rupert Hunt follow her with his men, who had been stationed at various tables throughout the jazz club as added protection. She hoped none of them saw tears gathering in her eyes. "Never let them see you cry," Mona mumbled to herself. "Don't give them that satisfaction."

Was Scott right?

Was she losing Robert Farley to a twenty-year-old girl?

22

Mona was going on her seventeenth hour of sleep and still shut up in her room.

Violet softly knocked on Mona's bedroom door. "Miss Mona, time to get up. You've slept all day. You need to eat something." She quietly opened the door and found Mona still asleep. Violet picked up Mona's evening gown, hung it up, and tiptoed out of the room.

Worried, Violet wanted to call a doctor, but Samuel stopped her. "Leave Miss Mona be, Violet. She's sleeping off her grief. That's nothing a doctor can do for her."

"Maybe Scott drugged her?"

"You know that's not the problem. Let her sleep. It's healing."

Earlier in the day, Rupert Hunt had told them

both what Scott had said to Mona about Robert Farley.

"I was close enough to hear the entire conversation. He worked her over about Farley, but she never broke script. Mona stayed focused, even when Scott was cruel. I swear he was trying to break her spirit."

"Maybe he did," Violet suggested. "Miss Mona hasn't been out of her bedroom since she came back from the club."

"Mona's a tough cookie. She'll work this out on her own. I say leave her alone," advised Hunt.

So that's what Violet, Samuel, and Jamison did. They let Mona sleep.

Sleuthing on their own, Violet and Samuel purchased more London newspapers and tabloids, and they were not happy with what they read. Lord Farley was now officially Duke of Brynelleth and according to the papers, he was keeping company with Lady Imogene, who was acting as hostess of Brynelleth.

"What should we do?" Violet asked.

Samuel advised, "Act normal and don't bring up Lord Farley. Let's carry on as normal. When Miss Mona wakes up, she'll be very hungry, so

I'm going to make a real Southern meal—pinto beans with onions, greens, and cornbread washed down with buttermilk."

"I don't think Miss Mona cares for buttermilk."

Samuel winked. "But I do."

Violet chuckled.

"What's funny?"

"I was just thinking about something Mrs. Longworth said to me a few weeks ago when I ordered corn mush for lunch. 'You can take the girl out of the South, but not the South out of the girl!'"

"She was right, wasn't she?"

With a lopsided grin, Violet said, "I do believe so because my mouth is watering at the mere mention of that meal, Samuel. Makes me think of home. I miss it so."

"Let's get to it then. I'll send Jamison out for vittles. By tonight, we will have a feast to eat."

Five hours later, Mona awoke to the aroma of fried catfish, stewed okra and tomatoes, pinto beans, and freshly baked cornbread wafting through her bedroom. She took a shower and washed her hair. Putting on slacks and a soft top, she opened her bedroom door to find Jamison, Samuel, and Violet at a little card table in the drawing room eating off the hotel's fine china.

Violet jumped up. "Miss Mona. We were just having supper."

Blinking, Mona glared at them, making the three feel uncomfortable.

Jamison and Samuel glanced at each other, wondering if Mona was angry.

"THAT'S IT!" Mona cried, suddenly. "The solution I've been looking for. I'm going to give a dinner party!"

23

"I don't know, Mona. You're asking a lot," Alice Longworth replied.

"You owe me. I wouldn't be in this mess if it wasn't for you."

"That's rude of you. You wanted to meet your idol Eleanor Roosevelt, and you did because of me."

"I wasn't aware that having lunch with the First Lady would put me in proximity to the cloak and dagger gents, who are having a great time at my expense. Mrs. Roosevelt gave my name to William Donovan. He wants me to become the next Mata Hari."

Alice scoffed. "That woman was overrated."

"Yeah, she was killed by a firing squad. I don't want that to become my fate."

"Mona, you're being ridiculous. I know Bill. He's not asking you to become a real spy or a mole. He only wants a little information if you should stumble across it."

Mona picked at her sandwich. She and Alice were having tea in Alice's garden as a maid poured hot liquid into delicate fine china cups. Mona peered at the china. "This looks like your father's presidential china."

"Oh, does it?"

Mona picked up a plate, studying it. "I've seen pictures of your father's china and this design is a dead ringer for President Theodore Roosevelt's official White House china."

Alice placed several cucumber sandwiches on the plate Mona was holding toward her. "There. Now you won't have to look at it."

"Alice, you've been stealing your father's china from the White House!" Mona broke off into peals of laughter. "Oh, you are so precious."

"I was afraid Eleanor was going to find some excuse to get rid of it."

"She can't. The china belongs to the American people. We paid for it."

"I tell you that she is systemically getting rid

of Father's presidential china."

"Now, look who is being ridiculous."

Mona nibbled on a sandwich. "I'll tell Eleanor if you don't help me."

"You're blackmailing me?"

Mona thought for a second. "Yes, I am."

Alice threw her napkin on the metal table in a huff.

"Come on, Alice. It will be fun. You like gossip, intrigue, and tweaking the noses of the Washington elite. This is right up your alley."

"It could backfire badly for the both of us."

"That's what makes it so much fun."

"Mona, I must tell you since Robert has taken his father's title, he can't marry you for at least a year. This makes you less valuable to men like Bill Donovan. He might not be interested in pursuing you further. Have you heard from Robert?"

Mona shook her head.

"I hate to be cruel, but there it is. I know Robert loves you, but he has other considerations now. He has to think of his position and the future of the Farley blood line. Robert can't go running off to Kentucky whenever he feels like it."

"You make it sound like we are a pair of breeding horses. Look Alice, this isn't about Robert. It's about Moon Enterprises and the copper mines. I feel these men are maneuvering me out of the picture to get their hands on the Moon copper ore. Aunt Melanie would be more pliable if in charge. I must stay in control. We have come so far in just a short time. I can't have Melanie undo everything just to make a profit at the expense of the workers and give these buyers carte blanche. I must stay as head of Moon Enterprises."

"I'm not sure who you are talking about. If these men are Americans and want the blasted copper ore, just sell it to them. That's why you are in business."

"That's the problem, Alice. I don't know who the bad guys and the good guys are. I need to pin them down. I want to know that I am selling to buyers who won't use the copper against the United States, and I require you to help me to do it."

"Very well. It sounds like my patriotic duty is to assist you. I hope you appreciate all I do for you."

Mona sighed with relief. "And I promise not to tell anyone that you are filching china from the White House in return."

Alice sniffed. "You are such a miserable creature."

Mona blew Alice a kiss. "Takes one to know one." She happily put a poppy seed muffin on her plate as well as more scones. Catching sight of her "Jungle Red" painted fingernails, Mona was so glad she had claws and knew how to use them.

And she was going to scratch some ornery cusses tomorrow night.

24

Samuel answered the door to Alice Longworth's home. "Good evening. May I see your invitation, please?"

Ambassador Lindsay said, "I am an old friend of Mrs. Longworth's. You must be new."

"Your invitation, please."

Flabbergasted, Lindsay looked at his wife. "This is most unusual."

Not wishing to cause a fuss, Lady Lindsay reached for the invitation in her purse. After receiving it by special courier that morning, she dared not refuse to accept, realizing the dinner was going to be a showdown of sorts. She prayed she was not going to be one of Mona's targets. Seeing her husband's confusion, Lady Lindsay was glad her husband didn't have a clue about the true intent of this night's gathering. Wondering who else might be attending, she handed the invitation to Samuel, who read it out loud.

Mrs. Nicholas Longworth hereby requests that you honor us with your presence for dinner to celebrate Mona Moon, one of America's most esteemed women. Drinks at eight sharp. Declines will not be accepted. You better come if you know what's good for you.

"Let me see that," Sir Lindsay said, snatching the invitation out of Samuel's hands and reading it twice. "Good grief. Alice has finally gone off her rocker. Imagine writing an invitation like this. It sounds almost threatening."

"It's one of Alice's little jokes, dear. Let's go in." Lady Lindsay gently wrapped her arm around her husband's arm. "Ready?"

Sir Lindsay acquiesced. "I hope this is not going to be a surprise party. It's not my birthday, is it?"

Lady Lindsay looked tenderly at her distinguished-looking husband dressed in his best tux. Only the best would do for Alice. "No, my love. That's several months away."

Samuel widened the door and allowed the couple to enter before taking their wraps.

Dressed in an organdy, pale pink sheath over a dark pink gown, Violet greeted each guest. "Cocktails are being served in the drawing room. Please follow me."

Irritated, Sir Lindsay said, "I know the way, young lady. I have been a guest in this house before you were born."

Violet said, "Ambassador, I have been given strict instructions to announce each guest. Please, sir."

Lindsay stopped in the hallway. "What is going on?"

"Thank you, sir." Violet scooted around the Lindsays in the hallway and opened the double doors. "Ambassador Lindsay and Lady Lindsay." She waited until they had passed through before she closed the drawing room doors again.

"Two more to go," Samuel said, clicking off his list.

"Do you think they'll come?"

"I would, just out of curiosity."

Violet giggled, putting her hand over her mouth, fearful that the guests in the drawing room might hear her. But she needn't have worried.

The guests only had eyes for Mona.

25

Mona was wearing a Grecian-style, off-one-shoulder, pleated linen dress with a gold head-dress and choker. "Good evening, Ambassador Lindsay and Lady Lindsay. So glad you could join us."

"It didn't seem like we had a choice. Perhaps you would like to introduce us to your other guests." Ronald suggested. He was very annoyed and thought the entire affair was odd.

Wearing her signature blue in a long velvet gown, Alice stepped forth. "Welcome. We are waiting for two more guests. Would you like a cocktail, you two?"

"A sherry for me," Lady Lindsay said. "Ronald?"

"Same here."

Jamison, who was tending bar, poured two small crystal glasses of sherry for the Lindsays.

Alice nervously rubbed her hands together. "You know Bill Donovan, of course."

Looking out the garden French doors, Donovan turned, "Hello, Ronald. Elizabeth. Haven't seen you since the embassy party."

Mona moved over to the next guest sitting on the couch. "This lovely lady is Nasha Martin."

"Very nice to meet you both," Martin said, looking a bit sad. No doubt she had been told of Otto Mueller's untimely death.

Mona explained, "Miss Martin is the newest songbird of Bluebird Records."

"Oh, you're a vocalist," Lady Lindsay remarked.

"Yes, I sing jazz and the blues. I hope to be as big as Bessie Smith."

Lady Lindsay said, "I'm afraid I'm not familiar with her."

"Don't bother. I've heard her and she sounds like a chicken squawking after its head has been cut off," Alice said.

Insulted, Nasha Martin said, "I beg to differ, Mrs. Longworth. Bessie Smith will go down as one of the great singers of the twentieth century, while many of your high-toned singers will be long forgotten. I know something about music and singers."

Donovan said, "I was always partial to Enrico Caruso. Now, he was a great tenor. I heard him perform at the Metropolitan Opera House." Donovan scratched his chin. "Oh, gosh, that was way back."

"He's been dead over ten years," Miss Martin said.

"A great loss. A great loss," Donovan said. "You know the Black Hand threatened to pour lye down Caruso's throat if he didn't pay protection money."

Nasha Martin recoiled in horror. "What happened?"

"Caruso paid them two thousand and then they wanted fifteen thousand, so he got the police involved. They staged a sting operation and caught the extortionists."

"I hope those men went to jail. What a dirty trick to do to a singer," Martin said passionately. "I don't know what I'd do if I were to lose my voice."

Mona moved to the man sitting in a chair next to the fireplace with his legs crossed. "Ambassador Lindsay and Lady Lindsay, this is Abraham Scott."

Mona intently watched their interaction.

The Lindsays nodded.

"I'm a great admirer of yours, Ambassador," Scott said.

"Thank you," Ronald cocked his head. "Have we met before, sir?"

"No, Ambassador. I'm afraid not."

"May I ask what you do?"

"I work for the United States government."

"In what capacity?"

"That's a great question, Ambassador," Mona said. "Yes, tell us, what you do, Honest Abe."

Before Scott could respond, Violet tapped on the drawing room door and opened it. "Presenting Lisa LaMour." Violet stepped back, allowing LaMour to strut into the room.

LaMour was wearing a nude color, form fitting, strapless dress glittering with rhinestones, mainly at the erogenous zones. Unlike most short bobs of the era, LaMour wore her shoulder length red hair down with a gardenia clip over her right ear.

Alice threw her hands over her face. "I'm blinded by the reflection of the light."

Ignoring Alice's sarcastic remark, Mona strode over to LaMour. "How nice of you to come."

"I can hardly turn down a free meal," LaMour teased, looking about the room. Seeing Ambassador Lindsay, she squealed, "RONNIE!"

Mona turned and shot an amused look at Alice, who shrugged.

Lindsay tugged at his collar and stood, taking Miss LaMour's hand. He kissed it in the continental manner. "Very nice to see you again, Miss LaMour. You remember my wife, Lady Lindsay."

LaMour did a small curtsy. "Nice to see you again, Lady Lindsay."

"I thought you'd be on your way to Hollywood by now, Miss LaMour," Lady Lindsay remarked.

"Next week. I was supposed to go this week, but there was some glitch with the tickets. So I'm stuck for the time being. I've got to say I find Washington to be a boring town. Nothing is ever going on. I would have rather waited in New York."

Alice stifled a laugh. Oh, what a treasure Lisa LaMour was!

"Have you visited the Capitol or the many museums Washington has to offer?" Lady Lindsay suggested.

"Why would I do that?" LaMour said. "This is not my country."

Bristling, Nasha Martin said, "And yet you wish to make your fortune here, taking income away from American artists."

"Money is money, whatever the country. Right?"

Mona moved to intercept. "Miss LaMour, may I introduce you to Abraham Scott?"

He nodded while looking the beautiful lady up and down.

"This is Mr. Donovan."

"Nice to meet you," LaMour said, curtsying.

"You don't have to curtsy. I'm an American," Donovan rebuked. He had seen Miss LaMour at the British Embassy party and thought her to be a beautiful tart.

Mona walked Miss LaMour toward Nasha Martin, who looked upon the ingénue with some distaste. "And this is Miss Martin."

The two women barely acknowledged each other.

Mona asked LaMour, "What would you like to drink?"

"Champagne if you have it."

"We do. Jamison, would you please pour Miss LaMour a flute of champagne?"

"Yes, Miss Mona. Coming up."

Lady Lindsay raised an eyebrow. Servants were not to reply to requests, but perform tasks in silence.

Donovan looked about the room. "You said there were two more guests coming. Miss LaMour has arrived."

"I think I heard the doorbell just now," Mona replied to Donovan. She knew her guests were getting impatient.

Violet opened the drawing room door and announced, "Mrs. Lars Dardel."

Mrs. Dardel entered the room holding out her invitation. She wore a severe black mourning dress, black stockings, and a widow's veil that covered her from head to chest. Mrs. Dardel dramatically lifted the dark veil. "What is the meaning of this? You'd better come if you know what's good for you. That invitation sounded like a threat."

Alice stepped forward. "I'm very sorry, Mrs. Dardel, but I had to make sure you'd accept."

Mrs. Dardel noticed Ronald and Elizabeth Lindsay. "Ambassador. Lady Lindsay. I'm surprised to see you. Why are we here?"

Mona clasped her hands together. "We are here to discuss Lars Dardel's death." She turned to Mrs. Dardel. "I'm going to announce who murdered your husband at tonight's dinner, Mrs. Dardel."

Mrs. Dardel's face drained of color and then she fainted.

26

Samuel brought smelling salts as the men lifted Mrs. Dardel into a chair. Alice, Lady Lindsay, and Nasha Martin stood to one side as Mona administered the smelling salts. Lisa LaMour sat disinterested in a chair, sipping on her drink.

"I'm so sorry," apologized Mrs. Dardel, looking up at Mona. "I thought you said you were going to announce the murderer of my husband."

"I am, Mrs. Dardel. I just need to round out a few facts first."

"I won't stand for this," Mrs. Dardel said.

"I don't see why not. At the funeral you said some pretty harsh things about the murder of your husband being hushed up and glossed over. I'm giving you a chance to participate in discovering the identity of his killer. Isn't that what you want? Justice for Lars."

Confused, Mrs. Lars looked around at the people in the room. "I don't see how that will happen. I don't know who these people are, except for the Ambassador and his wife."

Mona said, "That's where you're wrong. Everyone here played a part in your husband's death."

"I most certainly did not!" Donovan said indignantly. He made his way to the door when he found it locked.

"All the doors have been locked, Mr. Donovan," Mona said. "And there are guards posted outside. I'm afraid everyone is going to stay until I am finished."

"Is this like a screen test?" LaMour asked, standing up and looking around. "Is there a Hollywood agent watching from a peephole?" She went over to a wall mirror and looked behind it.

"I'm afraid this is real, dear. Please sit back down. This may take a while."

"I don't see why I'm being dragged into this," Donovan said.

"If you bear with me, it will become clear," Mona said.

"Does this mean there is no dinner?" Miss Martin asked. "I'm famished, and I have a set to sing at eleven."

Scott laughed and stretched out his long legs. "I, for one, am intrigued. Sleuth away, Miss Mona. Give Miss Marple a run for her money."

"Thank you, Abraham. My involvement with Lars Dardel's death began with my request of Alice Longworth for an invitation to the White House. I have long been an admirer of Eleanor Roosevelt. When Alice was informed of my coming east, she wangled a luncheon invitation with the First Lady. I think the First Lady agreed to this luncheon when she learned of the Moon copper mines. She wanted to meet me and see where I stood on world affairs. It was a test of sorts. It seemed that I passed because Mrs. Roosevelt gave my name to William Donovan."

"Be careful, Miss Moon," Donovan cautioned. "Remember our pact."

"Why did she do that?" asked Nasha Martin.

"Because Mr. Donovan is interested in the purchase of copper as is Mr. Scott."

Relieved that Mona was not disclosing his real connection to the White House, Donovan nodded. "That's right."

"But Mr. Scott and Mr. Donovan weren't the only ones interested in copper ore. Lars Dardel was interested as well. He approached me at the embassy ball to sell copper ore to Sweden, but he wouldn't tell if he was acting officially on behalf of the Swedish government. Do you know anything about Lars' desire for copper ore, Mrs. Dardel?"

Mrs. Dardel dabbed her forehead with her perfumed handkerchief. "I didn't." She turned to Lady Lindsay. "Isn't it very hot in here?"

Mona continued. "No, I don't think you did know that your husband was trying to procure copper."

"Where's this going?" Lady Lindsay demanded.

"There was another dynamic happening that coincided with my trip here." Mona looked around the room. "And that was the death of Alburn Bower, who died two doors down from me on the second floor of the Willard Hotel."

Mona noticed that Scott and Donovan looked uncomfortable.

"Who is he?" LaMour asked.

"Alburn Bower was a jazz lover whose alias was Otto Mueller."

Nasha Martin gasped. "Otto died on the SS Cathay. He was drunk and fell overboard. That's what I was told." She gave Scott a heated stare.

Mona shook her head. "No, Nasha. That's not how he died. Otto Mueller was a translator working at the German Embassy. He had access to cables, letters, and telegrams coming into the German Embassy. He disliked the Nazi party and was selling their secrets to the Swedish government. That's where Lars Dardel comes in. Lars was a Nazi collaborator and sympathizer. He knew that Mueller was carrying papers that were potential dynamite. If Lars could get those papers, he could prove to Ambassador Boström that Germany has plans to aggressively build their military back up and ignore the Treaty of Versailles."

Alice said, "Why would Lars Dardel pursue exposing that information if he was pro-Nazi? The Swedes are neutral."

"Are they? Officially yes, but I think they are waiting to see which way the wind blows," Mona said.

"He lied to me," Miss Martin said. "He didn't even tell me his real name."

"I think this Otto Mueller did love jazz and thought you were a great talent, but he used the club as a venue to dispense information about the Nazis."

Martin asked, "How did Otto really die?"

"He was shot to death by a British agent, who also had heard rumors about these papers. Great Britain has long thought Hitler was lying when he said he wants peace. They had to be sure, so they sent this agent."

"What's this man's name?"

"I don't know," Mona lied. "But Mr. Mueller caught the agent in his room, and there was a tussle. That's when he was shot."

"Will this agent be arrested for murder?"

"I'm sorry, Nasha, but this agent was from MI6. There will be no arrest."

"I have no idea what MI6 is."

Donovan interrupted, "You're better off then, Miss Martin. You have a bright future ahead of you. Forget about this Alburn Bower, known to you as Otto Mueller. That man was not worth your time."

"Seems to me Otto was trying to do the right thing. He wanted to expose the rearmament." Nasha Martin turned to Ambassador Lindsay. "Did you give the orders to have my Otto murdered?"

"No, my dear, but I did know of sensitive information leaking from the German Embassy. We were actively pursuing who the source was. And so were the Germans."

"And there might be leaks in our embassy as well. We lost an important file," Lady Lindsay said, giving Mona a conspiratorial glance.

"Hush, Elizabeth," Ronald admonished.

"We're getting off track here," Mona said.

Mrs. Dardel said to Mona, "So, Lars' politics were to the far-right. Lots of people have faith in Hitler. He's exciting, dynamic. He stirs the blood. The world needs a new strong man with fresh ideas. I still don't see how all of this helps my poor Lars. You have said yourself that Lars did not obtain those papers. Sounds like he was nowhere near this Otto or Alburn, whatever you want to call him, when murdered."

"There are many moving threads that I'm trying to weave together, Mrs. Dardel. Please be patient."

"Go on then."

"After your husband's death, I was visited by Abraham Scott, who claimed he worked for President Roosevelt. He was a little vague on what he did, how, or why, but he made life miserable for me. He said he was acting on President Roosevelt's orders and that he wanted me to spy for the United States government. He said he was acting as a liaison for you, Mr. Donovan."

"Is that so?" Donovan said, turning his attention to Scott.

Furious, Scott said, "You're not supposed to expose me like this. This might be considered treason."

Mona laughed. "Oh, Scott, you are such a fake, but I do admire your chutzpah."

"What do you mean?"

"Not only do you not work for President Roosevelt, you're not even an American."

Scott looked cagily around the room, looking for an avenue of escape. "I have no idea of what you mean." He pointed a finger at Mona. "You're one crazy dame making ridiculous accusations like that. I am American as apple pie."

Mona explained, "American men use one utensil when they eat—usually a fork. You eat the continental way of using a fork turned upside down accompanied by a knife. Then there's the way you sit. American men spread their legs apart. I know it's a vulgar habit, but it's how they sit. European men keep their legs together and often cross their legs at the knees while sitting, like you are now."

Scott hastily uncrossed his legs. "Many Yanks eat the European way."

Alice stepped in. "Most Americans do not. You see, after the War of Independence from Great Britain, Americans wanted to do things differently from the old British customs—like driving on the left side of the road, horse racing clockwise, and using a fork and knife when eating. Only upper class Americans eat with both a fork and knife still, and I'm sure you have noticed that many of us still speak with a soft British accent. My cousin, Eleanor, still does. It grates on my nerves, but there it is."

"You can't prove a thing," Scott said, defiantly.

"I think the U.S. State Department might

when they have a word from Ambassador Lindsay." Mona turned to Nasha Martin. "Miss Martin, you told me that you were to spy on your jazz patrons. Who was your handler? Who gave you money for information?"

Angry and feeling like a fool, Martin threw out her arm and pointed at Scott, confirming what she had told Mona earlier. "He did! It was Abraham."

William Donovan looked startled and moved toward Scott with a quickness and agility that defied his age.

Scott jumped up and ran for the French doors leading out to the garden, but Lindsay and Donovan caught him, pinning him to the floor.

Mona leaned over Scott. "The fact is that you don't work for President Roosevelt. You never did. You just go around town posing as an American agent. You really are a German provocateur, sent over here to stir up trouble any way you can."

"He won't be causing any more trouble in the States once I make a few phone calls tonight," Lindsay said.

Lady Lindsay beamed with delight at her husband catching a foreign spy. She was so very proud of him.

Violet rushed in with Samuel hot on her heels. "Is there trouble, Miss Mona?"

"It would help if one of you would procure a stout rope."

Donovan, still holding down Scott, ordered Samuel, "Get a rope, man. There's got to be one somewhere."

"Here, use this," Alice said, taking off her belt. She handed it to Donovan. "You can tie his hands with it."

"Thank you, Alice," Donovan replied.

"Good idea," Samuel said, removing his pants belt. "Use this for his feet." He and Donovan tied Scott up and put him in a chair.

"How do I fit into all of this? I don't know anyone here except for the Lindsays and only to say hello," Lisa LaMour complained.

"I'm going to explain that in just a moment."

Alice plopped down into a chair. "We are waiting with bated breath. Do go on."

"I can't take much more of this. I want to go home," Mrs. Dardel said.

"Don't you want to know who killed your

husband, Mrs. Dardel?"

Mrs. Dardel pointed at Scott. "He did. You said he was a German provocateur."

"But I didn't say he killed your husband. Otto Mueller, Abraham Scott, Nasha Martin, Ambassador Lindsay were all playing the Great Game, but none of them are murderers, and none of them ordered the murder of your husband. Not even the man sent to steal Otto Mueller's papers wanted to kill him. It was an unfortunate incident."

"Then who?"

Mona turned to Ambassador Lindsay. "That file you were missing?"

"Yes?"

Mona could see Lady Lindsay tense up. "I stole that file."

Ambassador Lindsay looked perplexed. "That's impossible."

Mona lied, "No, it's not. I stole it the same way Alice steals files from President Roosevelt's desk when she's snooping."

Alice said, "Hey, I just helped catch a spy. Don't involve me in your double dealings with Ronald."

"I will never tell how I got that file, but you got it back. Right?"

"I guess I have to beef up my security at the Embassy."

"I guess you will, Ambassador, but my lips are sealed about it, except that the secret coroner's report stated that a left-handed person stabbed Lars Dardel." Mona turned to Mrs. Dardel. "If you remember, I was one of the first people to reach Lars after he had been attacked, but I didn't know at the time how he was injured. I do remember you distinctly sobbing several feet from his body in the cloakroom."

"I discovered his poor body."

"But how did you know that he was dead? Did you check for a pulse?"

"No. I didn't touch him."

"Lars could have passed out from drinking or even had a heart attack. I only knew he was dead after I checked for a pulse. Until Ambassador Lindsay turned Lars over, I didn't know he had been attacked. How did you know he was dead before I did?"

"I don't know. He just looked dead."

"Mrs. Dardel, you wear your watch on your right wrist."

"So?"

"Left-handed people wear their watches on their right. You are left-handed. I think this is what happened. Lars had a reputation for the ladies. I think he cheated on you every chance he got."

"I can concur with that," Nasha Martin said. "He was always on the make. He even tried with me."

"That's enough, Miss Martin. Let's not pour salt into the wound. This is going to be painful enough." Mona sat beside a trembling Mrs. Dardel. "I think you knew about Lars' liaisons. You saw Lars take me out onto the patio and thought he was having a rendezvous with me. Then you witnessed him dancing with Miss LaMour and saw his hand fondle her backside."

"I should have slapped his face for that," LaMour insisted.

"Hush!" Alice admonished. "Mona's just getting to the good part."

Mona tried to be gentle. "I think you'd had enough and flew into a jealous rage. You stabbed Lars, Mrs. Dardel. You killed your own husband."

"Where's the knife?"

"I think you put it in your purse, Mrs. Dardel. The police were never called. I'm sure the Embassy did an in-house investigation. It was British soil, after all."

"I'm afraid when the staff did a second re-count of the silverware, we were missing a knife," Ambassador Lindsay said.

"My husband died of a heart-attack, did he not, Ambassador Lindsay? That's what was written in the papers," Mrs. Dardel uttered, staring into the fire. "It would look rather silly to have it come out now that he was murdered at your ball and on British soil right under your nose."

Taken back by Mrs. Dardel's effrontery, Lindsay had to concede. "Yes, Mrs. Dardel. It is as you say. Lars Dardel died of a heart attack."

"Thank you." Mrs. Dardel rose and made her way to the drawing room door.

Standing in front of the door, Violet and Samuel blocked her, looking at Mona.

Mona nodded and they moved away, allowing Mrs. Dardel free to leave.

Alice sputtered, "You're letting her go?"

Lindsay tried to calm Alice. "There's nothing we can do. It's a matter of British national security."

"But—" Alice said.

"No buts, just listen—all of you. This has to stay quiet. Tonight did not happen. In fact, I want the invitations from all of you," Lindsay said, holding his hand out. Everyone gave Lindsay their invitations as Jamison rummaged Scott's pockets for his.

"Aren't we even going to eat?" Lisa LaMour asked.

"I'll get you a doggy bag," Alice said.

Lindsay kissed Alice on the cheek. "You give one blast of a dinner party, Alice, you cheeky girl."

Lady Lindsay said to Alice, "We'll talk about this later."

Lindsay swirled on his wife. "No you won't. Tonight never happened. We were never here."

Lady Lindsay shrugged at Alice and followed her husband out of the house.

Scott struggled against his restraints as Alice asked William Donovan, "What should I do with him?"

"Let me make a phone call. My people will deal with him."

"Thanks," Alice said, gratefully.

Violet tugged on Mona's arm. "Who attacked me?"

Mona turned to Donovan. "Mr. Donovan?"

"It wasn't me."

Mona kicked Scott's foot. "I think it was you. After all, you were ordered to do mischief. I wouldn't say yes, so you decided to send me a message through Violet. You wanted to teach me a lesson."

"I guess you'll never know."

Taking her cue from Mona, Violet went up to Scott and angrily kicked him in the shin several times.

"You're hurting me," Scott complained.

"Oh, really. You don't like to be hurt." Violet leaned into Scott's face. "Look what those bully boys did to my face. They could have marred me for life."

"For goodness sakes, Bill, get that creep out of my house," Alice said.

"With pleasure," Donovan said, grabbing Scott by the tux's collar and bringing him to his feet. He dragged Scott through French garden doors.

"This is terrible," Alice wailed, looking sad.

"We caught a spy and a murderer," Mona said, astonished at Alice's melancholy.

"And I can't tell a soul! How awful is that? One of the most astonishing nights of my life, and I can't repeat a word of it." Alice sank into a chair. "My life is misery."

Mona laughed and poured Alice a stiff gin and tonic.

"What do we do now, Miss Mona?" Violet asked.

Mona put her arms around Violet's shoulders and squeezed. "We are going home, Violet. That's what we are going to do."

27

As Mona was checking out of the hotel, a man bumped into her. Recognizing him as the British agent who jumped out of the Willard's dining room window, Mona momentarily froze.

"Excuse me, Miss Moon, but you've dropped your newspaper. There's a very interesting article on page five." The man handed Mona a folded *London Times* and tipped his hat before exiting the Willard.

Mona waited until she got into her car before she opened the paper. There between page five and six was a sealed envelope. She carefully opened it and took out the letter.

Darling, I hope my friend, Colonel Maynard Pickard, got this note to you somehow. He said he knew someone who could hand it off without the press knowing it. It has been a circus here with the reporters following me. They give me neither rest nor peace. I knew I could not contact you through regular channels, as they are often compromised for a little coin. The newspapers would make your life a misery, too. As soon as I straighten out matters here, I am coming home. I can't wait to hold you in my arms. My love always, R.

Alice Blue

Alice blue is a pale shade of gray-blue associated with Alice Roosevelt Longworth as it was her signature color. The song, *Alice Blue Gown*, premiered in the 1919 Broadway musical *Irene*. The color is used by the United States Navy for the insignia and trim on the USS Theodore Roosevelt.

Alice Roosevelt Longworth (1884-1980)

Alice was the eldest child of U.S. President Theodore Roosevelt. Interested in politics, she married Nicholas Longworth (Republican-Ohio) who was the Speaker of the U.S. House of Representatives from 1925 to 1931. Their marriage was unconventional, and both parties had affairs. Alice's only child, Paulina, was sired from an affair with Senator William Borah of Idaho. Paulina died from an overdose in 1955, leaving Alice to raise her granddaughter. Known as a great wit, Alice is famous for saying, "If you haven't got anything nice to say about anybody, come sit next to me." She said of her father's need for attention, "My father always wanted to be the corpse at every funeral, the bride at every wedding, and the baby at every christening."

American Isolationism

A popular 1930s social and political philosophy advocating American non-involvement in foreign military conflicts, especially Europe and Asia.

Bessie Smith (1894-1937)

Nicknamed the Empress of the Blues, Smith was a popular American blues and jazz singer during the 1920s and 1930s. Smith recorded for Columbia Records. She died in a car crash at the age of 43 in 1937.

Black Hand

The Black Hand was a criminal enterprise brought over to the United States by Sicilian immigrants during the 1880s. Their game was mainly extortion. The origins of the Black Hand can be traced to the Kingdom of Naples as early as the 1750s.

Church of Sweden

Most Swedes converted from Catholicism to the Lutheran faith during the Protestant Reformation during the 16th century. Church of Sweden was the state religion until 2000.

Dorothy L. Sayers (1893-1957)

Sayers was an English mystery writer best known for *The Nine Tailors,* featuring her protagonist, English aristocrat and amateur sleuth, Lord Peter Wimsey. She was also a classical scholar who translated Dante's *Divine Comedy.* Besides writing mysteries, Sayers wrote plays, poetry, and literary criticism. Although she distanced herself from feminism, *Gaudy Night* is considered the first feminist mystery, featuring Harriet Vane and Lord Peter Wimsey.

Dust Bowl Pneumonia

The Dust Bowl occurred in the Great Plains when the top soil dried out and blew away causing gigantic dust clouds. This phenomenon was caused by drought and poor agricultural practices. Illnesses such as "dust pneumonia" results when humans and animals breathe in large quantities of dust, thus inflaming the alveoli and preventing the lungs from clearing. Symptoms include difficulty in breathing, chest pain, fever, and coughing. The Red Cross made and distributed dust masks during the Dust Bowl, but it is estimated 7000 people still died.

Eleanor Roosevelt (1884-1962)

Roosevelt served as First Lady of the United States from 1933 to 1945. During this time, Mrs. Roosevelt worked to expand the rights of working women, WWII refugees, and the civil rights of minorities. She advocated the U.S. join the United Nations and was appointed as its first delegate. Serving as first chair on the UN Commission on Human Rights, she oversaw the drafting of the Universal Declaration of Human Rights. Roosevelt later chaired President John Kennedy's Presidential Commission on the Status of Women. She was the niece of President Theodore Roosevelt and first cousin to Alice Roosevelt Longworth. Roosevelt married her fifth cousin once removed, Franklin Delano Roosevelt, who became the 32nd President of the U.S. She is considered one of the most admired people of the twentieth century.

Elizabeth Sherman Lindsay (1885-1954)

Lindsay was a noted landscape gardener and planted the gardens at the newly built British Embassy in Washington, D.C. She was married to the British diplomat Sir Ronald Lindsay and was the grandniece of Civil War General William

T. Sherman. She also worked as a Red Cross executive during the Great War (WWI).

Emily Price Post (1872-1960)

Post was a wealthy socialite who wrote novels, travel books, and etiquette books. Her 1922 etiquette book, *Etiquette in Society, in Business, in Politics, and at Home,* became a bestseller and launched Post as an American icon. She became a national figure on deciding what "good taste" was. After 1931, Post did radio programs and newspaper columns on proper etiquette. *Etiquette in Society, in Business, in Politics, and at Home is* still in print.

Enrico Caruso (1873-1921)

Caruso was an acclaimed international sensation noted for his operatic tenor ability. He made 247 recordings from 1902 to 1920.

Gertrude Bell (1868-1926)

Bell was an English explorer, cartographer, and archaeologist of Syria, Mesopotamia, and Arabia. She and T. E. Lawrence helped the Hashemites establish dynasties in Jordan and Iraq. She played a major role in establishing the borders for Iraq and was instrumental in establishing the Iraqi Museum.

G-man
It is slang for an FBI agent.

Gloria Vanderbilt (1924-2019)
Vanderbilt was an heiress of the Vanderbilt family. She was the niece of Lady Furness, mistress of the Prince of Wales and is the mother to Anderson Cooper. Her aunt, Gertrude Vanderbilt Whitney, took Gloria's mother to court as an unfit mother for custody of Gloria in 1934. It created a stir coming on the heels of the Lindbergh baby kidnapping and murder. The aunt won the suit. Gloria grew up to become a designer and entrepreneur of upscale blue jeans and perfumes.

Great Depression (1929-1939)
The Great Depression was a world-wide phenomenon caused by the U.S. stock market crash in October 1929. The years 1931-1934 were the worst years of the Depression with an unemployment percentage rate of 15.9, 23.6, 24.9, 21.7 respectively, and even in 1940 unemployment

was fifteen percent. President FDR's New Deal programs such as the CCC and the WPA helped, but it wasn't until WWII that the country roared out of the Great Depression for good.

Harlem

As a neighborhood of New York City, it was named after Haarlem in the Netherlands in 1658. It was predominantly occupied by Jewish and Italian immigrants in the 19th century until African-Americans began moving to Harlem at the beginning of the 20th century. During the 1920s and 1930s, Harlem was the center of the Harlem Renaissance when many African-American artists, writers, and performers congregated there to live and work.

Henrietta Nesbitt

Henrietta Nesbitt was hired by Eleanor Roosevelt as a housekeeper and cook for the White House. The two of them modernized the White House kitchen, thus upgrading its sanitary standards. Mrs. Roosevelt worked with Mrs. Nesbitt to create dishes that were nutritious and inexpensive. The First Lady believed the White House should provide an example during the Great

Depression and eat what the "people" ate. Lavish meals, even for State dinners, became a thing of the past in favor of more spartan meals. While nutritious, Mrs. Nesbitt's meals were not tasty, and the White House became known for its inedible food. The rule of thumb was to eat before you dined at the White House.

House of Saxe-Coburg and Gotha

A German dynasty founded by Ernest Anton, sixth duke of Saxe-Coburg-Saalfed. In Great Britain, the Saxe-Coburgs were descendants of (German) Albert, Prince Consort of (British) Queen Victoria (House of Hanover). In 1917, complaints about the British royal family's German surname caused King George V to change the name to the House of Windsor.

Jazz

Jazz is a variety of music originated by African-American musicians in New Orleans, Louisana around the turn of the 20th century. It was considered controversial when it spilled over into the white population as it was rumored to have begun in houses of ill repute. Jazz has its roots in ragtime and the blues.

Jean Harlow (1911-1937)

Harlow was an American comedic actress and one of the first sex symbols of the "talkies." Known as the "Platinum Bombshell", she became one of Hollywood's biggest stars and is still ranked at No. 22 on AFI's greatest female stars of the Golden Age of Hollywood. Harlow died of kidney failure at the age of twenty-six.

John Barrymore (1882-1942)

Barrymore was considered the greatest actor of his generation. He was known as "The Great Profile" because of his prominent nose. He is the grandfather of Drew Barrymore.

Lady Thelma Furness (1904-1970)

Lady Furness was the mistress of the Prince of Wales, later King Edward VIII, preceding Wallis Simpson. Her identical twin, Gloria, was the mother of Gloria Vanderbilt and the grandmother of Anderson Cooper.

Longworth Family

A distinguished family from Cincinnati, Ohio, who made their money from wine. Nicholas Longworth I is remembered as the father of

American wine making. Patrons of the arts, they donated land for parks and the Cincinnati Art Museum. Maria Longworth created the Rookwood Pottery Co. Nicholas Longworth III became Speaker of the House and married Alice Roosevelt. His campaigning for William Howard Taft on the Republican ticket for president, while Theodore Roosevelt also ran for president, caused an irreparable rift in their marriage.

Mata Hari (1876-1917)

Hari was a Dutch exotic dancer who was executed by a French firing squad for spying for Germany during the Great War (WWI).

Mesopotamia

Name for the historical region between the Tigris-Euphrates river system. Also called the Fertile Crescent. Name covers the modern countries of Kuwait, Iraq, Syria, and Turkey. The area is now referred to as the Middle East which also includes Egypt, Sudan, Saudi Arabia, and other countries.

MI6

MI6 or the Secret Intelligence Service (SIS) is the

foreign intelligence service of the United Kingdom. Founded in 1909 as part of the Secret Service Bureau, its duties expanded during WWI and adopted its current name in 1920. The SIS was not officially acknowledged until 1994 when the Intelligence Service Act of 1994 (ISA) was introduced to Parliament. And yes, like James Bond, MI6 agents do have a license to kill.

Mickey

Also known as a Mickey Finn. A drink spiked with a drug unbeknownst to the drinker.

Mint Julep

A bourbon, sugar, mint, and shaved ice concoction served in a sterling cup. It is associated with the Kentucky Derby and Kentucky. Recipe–1 oz bourbon, 1 tsp of granulated sugar, and water. Pour into a silver cup with fresh mint leaves over shaved ice.

Nineteenth Amendment (Amendment XIX) to the US Constitution

The 19th Amendment to the United States Constitution prohibits the states and the federal government from denying the right to vote to citizens of the United States on the basis of sex. It needed thirty-six states to pass the amendment, and Tennessee was the last state of the thirty-six to do so with only one vote passing it. Harry Burn, who was anti-suffrage for women, received a note from his mother, Phoebe Ensminger Burn, stating, "Hurrah, and vote for suffrage," and implored him to be a "good son." Harry did what his mother wanted and cast the last vote for suffrage breaking the tie. The amendment was adopted in 1920 but was challenged by Leser v Garnett and Fairchild v Hughes. Some states refused to vote on the amendment while other states, mostly in the South, rejected it. States would reverse their rejection of the amendment in favor of it as late as 1984. One vote *can* make all the difference. Thank you, Mrs. Burn, for sending that note to your son.

Oswald Mosley, 6th Baronet (1896-1980)

Mosley was leader of the British Union of Fascists (BUF). He was imprisoned in 1940 and the BUF was banned. He was released in 1943. Ruined and disgraced, Mosley was rejected for political office post WWII. He moved to France in 1951 for the remainder of his life.

Paul von Hindenburg (1847-1934)

Hindenburg was a German general and war hero who led the German Army during the Great War (WW1). In 1925, he became President of the German Weimar Republic until his death in August of 1934. He was instrumental in the Nazi rise to power in Germany, when he was forced to appoint Adolf Hitler as Chancellor of Germany. After Hindenburg died, Hitler combined the presidency and the chancellorship into one office with "führer" as the title for the new office. By September, Nazi control of Germany would be complete.

Shirley Temple Drink

Named after the popular child star of the 1930s, a Shirley Temple is a non-alcoholic drink traditionally made with ginger ale and grenadine, served with a maraschino cherry.

Sir Richard Burton (1821-1890)

Burton is best known as a British explorer searching for the source of the Nile and visiting Mecca in disguise when Europeans were forbidden to enter. Burton was a cartographer, author, translator, and an ethnographer. It is claimed that he spoke twenty-nine languages. He publicly criticized the colonial policies of the British Empire.

Sir Ronald Charles Lindsay (1877-1945)

Ambassador to the United States from 1930 to 1939. Lindsay was an Americanophile, who married two American women. After his first wife died in 1918, he married another American. Both women were grandnieces of Civil War General William Tecumseh Sherman. To change American's antiwar sentiment over to helping Great Britain, Lindsay hosted the 1939 Royal Garden Party for King George VI and Queen Elizabeth (Queen Elizabeth II's mother). The party was very controversial, but was considered the social event of the year, so everyone went. The King and Queen's visit was the beginning of an overt attempt to bridge stronger relations between the two countries.

T. E. Lawrence (1888-1935)

Known as Lawrence of Arabia, Lawrence was a British army officer, diplomat, and writer known for his role in the Arab Revolt (1916-1918) against the Ottoman Empire, which had sided with Germany during the Great War (WWI). He is professionally associated with Gertrude Bell.

Theodore Roosevelt (1858-1919)

He was the 26th president (1901-1909) of the United States. He was known for saying "Walk softly and carry a big stick" which was based on an African proverb—"Walk softly and carry a big stick. You'll go far." This was the basis of Roosevelt's foreign policy to appear benign, but to use force if necessary when national interests are threatened. He is known as a conservationist and created the United States Forest Service, thereby, establishing 150 national forests, 51 federal bird reserves, 4 national game preserves, and 5 national parks. During his residency, Roosevelt protected 230 million acres of public land. In 1916, President Woodrow Wilson would continue Roosevelt's work by creating the National Park Service. As for his daughter, Alice Roosevelt Longworth, Roosevelt said, "I can be President of the United States or I can control Alice. I cannot possibly do both."

Wallis Simpson (1896-1986)

Simpson was an American socialite, who began

an affair with Edward David Windsor, Prince of Wales, and heir to the British throne in 1934. After Wallis' divorce, her beau, now Edward VIII, King of United Kingdom, created a constitutional crisis when he announced his intention to marry the twice-divorced Mrs. Simpson. He abdicated the throne in 1936 in order to marry her. Both Simpson and the abdicated Edward VIII, now Duke of Windsor, were Nazi sympathizers and of great concern to the British government during WWII. The British went at great length to suppress intelligence from them. Prime Minister Winston Churchill even threatened the Duke with a court-martial if he did not follow orders from the British Government. Eventually, the Duke was appointed Governor of the Bahamas to get him and Simpson out of the Government's hair. After the war, the couple lived in France until their deaths. Simpson is attributed with the quote, "You can never be too rich or too thin."

Weimar Republic

Germany existed as a constitutional republic beginning in 1918 after the abdication of Kaiser Wilhelm and ended with President Paul Hindenburg's appointment of Adolf Hitler as chancellor in 1933. Thus Germany began its road to a dictatorship with the Nazis banning unions, other political parties, and a free press finally leading to WWII and genocide.

William Donovan (1883-1959)

Donovan was an American soldier, lawyer, and intelligence officer. Donovan is the only veteran to receive all four of the United States highest awards—the Medal of Honor, the Distinguished Service Cross, the Distinguished Service Medal, and the National Security Medal plus the Silver Star and the Purple Heart. He is best known for serving as the head of the Office of Strategic Services (OSS) during WWII. Another famous alumnus of the OSS was French gourmet chef, Julia Child. The OSS evolved to become the Central Intelligence Agency (CIA) after 1945. Donovan was recruited by President Roosevelt in 1934 to "casually" collect information against Nazis living in the U.S. as the States did not have a formal protocol as spying was frowned upon. Secretary of State Henry L. Stimson, under President Hoover, wrote in his memoirs, "Gentlemen do not read each other's mail," and pulled funding for intelligence gathering. Roosevelt knew that Donovan was a loud critic of such action and felt the U.S. needed a formal intelligence department like the United Kingdom's MI6. As soon as the U.S. was attacked in 1941, Roosevelt demanded that he be granted money for such a department with Donovan heading it. Thus began the OSS. Years later, Donovan died after acquiring dementia, taking all his secrets with him to the grave. A statue of Donovan stands in the CIA Headquarters lobby.

Willard Hotel (1847 –)

The Willard Hotel is a historic Beaux-Arts hotel in Washington, DC, where all the "swells" still stay. It is at this hotel that Kentuckian "The Great Compromiser" Henry Clay (1777-1852) introduced Kentucky bourbon to make Mint Juleps. He would bring a barrel from home to each legislative session and ask members from both parties to join him at the Willard for a Mint Julep. How do you think he was able to make members of Congress compromise over legislature? Perhaps over a Mint Julep drink?

Wollmar Boström (1878-1956)

Boström was a bronze medal 1908 Olympic tennis winner and Swedish ambassador in Washington, D.C. from 1925 to 1945.

Working Girls

1930s slang synonymous with prostitutes.

Other Books By Abigail Keam

Mona Moon Mysteries

Princess Maura Tales

Josiah Reynolds Mysteries

Last Chance For Love Series

About The Author

Abigail Keam is an award-winning and Amazon best-selling author. She is a beekeeper, loves chocolate, and lives on a cliff overlooking the Kentucky River. Besides the 1930s Mona Moon Mysteries, she writes the award-winning *Josiah Reynolds Mysteries*, *The Princess Maura Tales* (fantasy) and the *Last Chance For Love Series* (sweet romance).

Don't forget to leave a review! Tell your friends about Mona.

Thank you again, gentle reader, for your reviews and your word of mouth, which are so important for any book. I hope to meet you again between the pages.